D0482504

NO LONGER PROPERTY OF
GLENDALE LIBRARY,
ARTS & CULTURE DEPT.

GLENDALE PUBLIC LIBRARY
222 East Harvard St.
Glendale, CA 91205

THE TENTH LIFE

NO LONGER PROPERTY OF
GLENDALE LIBRARY,
ARTS & CULTURE DEPT.

MYSTERIES BY RICHARD LOCKRIDGE

The Tenth Life
A Streak of Light
Dead Run
Or Was He Pushed?
Death on the Hour
Not I, Said the Sparrow
Write Murder Down
Something Up a Sleeve
Death in a Sunny Place
Inspector's Holiday
Preach No More

Twice Retired
Troubled Journey
A Risky Way to Kill
Die Laughing
A Plate of Red Herrings
Murder in False-Face
With Option to Die
Murder for Art's Sake
Squire of Death
Murder Can't Wait
Murder Roundabout

OTHER BOOKS BY RICHARD LOCKRIDGE

One Lady, Two Cats
A Matter of Taste

The Empty Day
Encounter in Key West

Mr. and Mrs. North

BOOKS BY FRANCES AND RICHARD LOCKRIDGE
MR. AND MRS. NORTH

Murder by the Book
Murder Has Its Points
The Judge Is Reversed
Murder Is Suggested
The Long Skeleton
Voyage into Violence
Death of an Angel
A Key to Death
Death Has a Small Voice
Curtain for a Jester
Dead as a Dinosaur
Murder Comes First
The Dishonest Murderer

Murder Is Served
Untidy Murder
Death of a Tall Man
Murder Within Murder
Payoff for the Banker
Killing the Goose
Death Takes a Bow
Hanged for a Sheep
Death on the Aisle
Murder Out of Turn
A Pinch of Poison
The Norths Meet Murder
Murder in a Hurry

CAPTAIN HEIMRICH

The Distant Clue
First Come, First Kill
—With One Stone
Show Red for Danger
Accent on Murder
Practise to Deceive
Let Dead Enough Alone
Burnt Offering

Death and the Gentle Bull
Stand Up and Die
Death by Association
A Client Is Canceled
Foggy, Foggy Death
Spin Your Web, Lady
I Want to Come Home
Think of Death

MYSTERY ADVENTURES

The Devious Ones
Quest of the Bogeyman
Night of Shadows
The Ticking Clock
And Left for Dead
The Drill Is Death

The Golden Man
Murder and Blueberry Pie
The Innocent House
Catch as Catch Can
The Tangled Cord
The Faceless Adversary

CATS
Cats and People

MAR 1 7 1978

THE TENTH
LIFE

by Richard Lockridge

M

J. B. Lippincott Company
Philadelphia and New York

Copyright © 1977 by Richard Lockridge
All rights reserved
First edition
Printed in the United States of America
10 9 8 7 6 5 4 3 2 1

U.S. Library of Congress Cataloging in Publication Data

Lockridge, Richard, birth date
  The tenth life.

  I. Title.
PZ3.L81144Te   [PS3523.0245]   813'.5'2   77–6673
ISBN–0–397–01237–3

For Hildy

THE TENTH LIFE

1

It was a few minutes after six in the afternoon, and the afternoon was in mid-July. Across the Hudson, the sun was declining, but not hurrying about it. When they had come out of the house and onto the terrace, the temperature had been 94. Possibly it was, this half hour later, down to 92.

Inspector M. L. Heimrich, New York State Police, and Susan Heimrich would have been cooler in the house, with the air conditioning on. They were quite aware of this. They could have sat by the big west window and watched the sparkle of the declining sun on the wide river. Oh, not as well as here on the terrace, partly in the shade of the big ash tree. That shade would not last long. When the sun got a little lower, its rays would slant under the ash's lowest branches. Eventually, it would dazzle into their eyes. Already it was reaching Mite. The big black cat, who had so absurdly outgrown his name, twitched his skin, to make the too-hot sun go away.

It didn't work. Mite stretched, without getting up. Then he got up and stretched again. Then he moved a foot or two into deeper shade and lay down to rest. He did not curl. He lay stretched to his full length.

"He's really a very long cat, isn't he?" Susan Heimrich said and swished the gin and tonic in her glass so that the ice tinkled.

Merton Heimrich made the appropriate response, which was "Mmm." He added to it. "Remember when Colonel—?" He did not finish, since there was no need to finish. It would have been foolish to finish, since of course they both remembered the day their Great Dane had come home from somewhere with a small, wet and indignant black kitten in his mouth and put it down on the terrace flagstones for their approval. And got his nose scratched for his trouble.

"Where is that damn dog?" Heimrich said, not as a question to be answered. Susan merely shook her head.

She looks cool, Heimrich thought. How does she manage it? Of course, that scant dress she's wearing leaves a lot of her exposed to what stirring of air there is. A stirring, of course, from the southwest. Which meant that the weather forecast almost certainly was right. "Hot and humid through Sunday, with a chance of afternoon and evening thundershowers." The same forecast as for this Saturday, although as yet no thundershowers, and no sign of any on the way. But here, miles above the city, in Van Brunt, Putnam County, New York, the temperature would edge down after sunset. Well, after ten o'clock, anyway. At least they weren't in the city. And tonight they would leave the air conditioning on, for the first time this summer.

"Possibly chasing rabbits," Susan said. "Although not so much anymore. He's getting along, Merton. Like—" She did not finish that, because of the way her husband looked at her. It was not the look of a man who thinks his wife is getting on, or looking it.

"They're not a long-lived breed," Heimrich said. "I read that somewhere, didn't I?"

"Possibly, dear. The purebreds, anyway. The show types. They pretty much bred the insides out of them. To make them what the judges call 'proper conformity.' Which, with Danes, seems to mean thin in the middle. Yes, mutts tend to live longer. And Colonel must be getting on for—"

She did not finish. The big Great Dane named Colonel came through a gap in a stone fence a hundred yards or so from the terrace. It was a fence which Colonel had usually jumped; jumped, anyway, until a year or so before.

And, crossing the field toward the terrace, the big dog had bounded. Until a year or so ago, anyway. Now he walked slowly, as if it were a great effort to walk at all. The old boy is getting to be a very old boy, Heimrich thought. Of course, it's a very hot afternoon. This kind of humid heat takes it out of everybody.

He handed Susan a lighted cigarette. He lighted one for himself. Her glass was still half full; his own was lower. But there was no hurry about it. On this mid-July Saturday there was no hurry about anything. There had not even been much hurry at the barracks of Troop K. In the city, violence flared in hot weather. Not so much here in the country. Except, of course, violence by motorcar, which was not—which usually was not—of immediate professional concern to Inspector M. L. Heimrich, Bureau of Criminal Investigation.

They watched Colonel coming toward them. He

11

was making heavy going of it, certainly; heavy, panty going. And his big head was drooping, as if it were too heavy for his high, thin body. He did not look up to see that they were waiting for him.

The terrace was less than a foot above the lawn the big dog was trudging over. But when Colonel came to this curb, he stopped and looked at it as if he had never seen it before; as if it had not been for years something to take in stride, something not to be noticed. Finally, he lifted one forepaw and then the other. His hind legs dragged as he climbed to the terrace—staggered to the terrace.

They were both watching him by then. Mite rolled to his feet to watch his friend, who was moving so unlike the way his friend usually moved.

On the terrace, but still not in the shade of the ash, Colonel lay down. With a thump, pretty much as always. For the big dog, lying down had always been a form of collapse. But, down on belly, he had always lifted his head to gaze at whatever was in front of him with sad, discouraged eyes. Life had always seemed to discourage Colonel, if one could accept the expression of his eyes.

This time he did not lift his head. He supported it on outstretched paws.

"The heat?" Susan said.

"Perhaps. If he's been running in the sun. Only—"

Susan, who was now sitting on the chaise she had been lying on, said, "Yes, I wonder too." She said, "Colonel?" to the dog who had been hers before he became theirs. Ten years ago? Had it really been that long? He had been not much more than a puppy when he came to live with a well-loved woman and an unknown man in the house above the Hudson, which once had been a barn. So, Colonel was over ten. A considerable age for a Dane.

12

Mite got up from the flagstones. He walked toward the collapsed dog. He walked slowly, cautiously. It was almost as if he were stalking his lifetime friend. When he was two feet or so from the prostrate dog, Mite stopped. He appeared to sniff the dog. Then he made a low, mewing sound and turned away. He walked to Merton Heimrich and sat and looked up at Heimrich. It was almost, Heimrich thought, as if the big black cat were asking a question, seeking to have something explained to him.

"Yes, Mite, I'm afraid so," Heimrich said and then, to Susan, who had left her chaise and was crouched beside her dog, "They always seem to know, don't they? When another of them is sick?"

"He's breathing," Susan said. "Just managing to, it feels like." She had a hand on the big dog's side. "The vet, dear. Maybe there'll be something he can do. Dr. Barton?"

There were two veterinarians within reasonable distance. Dr. Peabody was the nearer, but he was primarily a big animal man, a man for horses and cows. Cows are not too numerous in the vicinity of Van Brunt. There are more horses. A few miles south, just over the Westchester County line, there is even a hunt.

But the biggest dog does not constitute a "big animal" in veterinarian usage.

Adrian Barton, DVM, was another matter. He had a small animal hospital a few miles up NY 11F, a little their side of Cold Harbor. His patients were largely canine, although he accepted cats, of which some veterinarians are wary. Cats are inclined to die suddenly and unexpectedly. They are also almost certain to claw and, as opportunity offers, bite. No cat ever believes something unpleasant is being done for his own good. Dogs are more amenable. And their claws are not so sharp.

13

Also, Colonel had been to Dr. Barton's hospital once when he had mistakenly thought a porcupine might want to play.

Colonel had always enjoyed riding in an automobile, had always bounded through an opened car door and taken over the back seat. Heimrich backed the Buick as close to the terrace as was possible and opened its nearside door. Colonel heard the sound and, just perceptibly, raised his heavy head. Then he put it down on his paws again.

Merton Heimrich carried the heavy dog to the car. Heimrich is a big man. Susan let Mite into the house. She promised him that he would, eventually, be given dinner. Mite didn't believe a word of it and said so. It *was* time for Mite's dinner. It must be almost time for theirs. Susan looked at her watch. Not for theirs, not at six thirty.

Still, they had better make sure Dr. Barton was still at his hospital; still available. She looked in the telephone directory. "Barton A DVM." She dialed. She got the ringing signal; got it again and again. Probably Dr. Barton kept office hours; possibly, like some doctors who treated two-legged animals instead of those with four, veterinarians closed up shop on Saturdays. Some doctors of humans also took Wednesdays off. Like barbers, Susan thought, and let Barton's telephone ring on. After all, animals in a hospital would not be left totally untended. Surely—

"Dr. Barton's office. Can I help you?"

The voice was female. It was a young voice.

"Mrs. Heimrich," Susan said. "Mrs. M. L. Heimrich." The "M. L." might help. It denoted a State Police inspector. "We have a sick dog we'd like Dr. Barton to look at. Is the doctor there?"

There was a pause, apparently for reflection.

"Well, yes. But the office hours end at five. Anyway, I think he's operating. Of course, if it's an emergency, Mrs. Heimrich?"

"Yes," Susan said. "We're afraid it is. Can I speak to the doctor?"

"I can't interrupt him while he's operating. But, if it's really urgent, I suppose you can bring the dog along. Is it a big dog?"

"A Great Dane," Susan said, and got a tentative "Oh" for an answer. A "well" was added to it.

A very young voice, Susan thought. Almost a child's voice? A child timorous about the arrival of a Great Dane, who was not called "great" by accident?

"My husband can handle him," Susan said. "My husband's rather a big man, Miss—"

"Carol Arnold, Mrs. Heimrich. In—oh, about half an hour, I guess. Doctor ought to be finished by then. He's spaying a cat."

There seemed to be nothing to say to that except "In about half an hour, then." So Susan said it. She sidestepped Mite, who was rubbing against her ankles. Mite again spoke about dinner. This time, he got it.

"He's still alive," Merton Heimrich told her when she was back at the car. "Just barely, I'm afraid. Susan, I'm afraid—"

"Yes," Susan said. "So am I. I called the vet. He'll be expecting us. In about half an hour. If he's finished spaying a cat. I got his secretary. Or nurse, or something. She's going to tell him."

Heimrich drove the Buick down the steep drive, between the boulders; down the steep, winding blacktop called High Road to NY 11F, which there is still Van Brunt Avenue. When a car he is in starts to move, Colonel usually sticks his head out a window. This time he did not move; he lay stretched on the back seat.

15

But they could hear him breathing as they turned north toward Cold Harbor. It was gaspy breathing.

Heimrich did not drive fast. Cold Harbor was only about twenty minutes away; Dr. Barton's office was this side of Cold Harbor.

The sign said "Barton Lane," and it was on the right as they drove north. The lane was narrow and blacktopped. Heimrich turned the Buick into it. After a couple of hundred yards, the lane twisted sharply to the left. Then they came up to a low, rectangular brick building. Beyond it, but close to it, was a white frame house; a rather large house. A sign in front of the brick building read, SMALL ANIMAL HOSPITAL. ADRIAN BARTON, DVM.

It was Susan who went to the door of the small animal hospital; Merton opened a car door and regarded Colonel, who, this time, raised his head a little and opened his eyes. They were always sad eyes. This time they were sadder than ever, and Heimrich imagined there was a question in them.

"I don't know, old boy," Heimrich told the dog. Colonel closed his eyes again. It was, Heimrich thought, as if the big dog accepted an answer. Anyway, he was still alive, and he was certainly big. It wouldn't be easy to get him out of the car, unless the vet was inclined to give a hand, or to send somebody who could. Heimrich put a hand on the dog's head. Colonel twitched an ear.

There was a sign by the hospital door. It read "Ring and Walk In." Susan rang and tried the door. The sign was more encouraging than accurate. Susan rang again. This time she heard footfalls beyond the locked door. They were quick and light. And the door was opened.

It wasn't a child who opened. It was a young

woman, probably in her mid-twenties, or approaching them, and certainly very pretty. Her blond hair was softly smooth on her head and her blue eyes were noticeably large. She was wearing white slacks and a white tunic; she could have been a registered nurse in a hospital for humans. Her smile was almost as impersonal as an R.N.'s smile. She said, "I'm sorry. We keep it locked after five. Are you the one who called? About a sick Great Dane?"

"Susan Heimrich, yes. Is Dr. Barton ready to see us?"

"I'm sure he will be very soon," the girl said. "I'm Carol Arnold. I'm sort of helping Doctor out during the summer. Actually, I'm studying to be a veterinarian. At Cornell. I suppose you could say I'm kind of interning. You say the dog's a Great Dane?"

"Yes, Miss Arnold. Shall I have my husband bring him in?"

Susan looked around the air-cooled room as she went into it and, vaguely, remembered it from the porcupine time. It had been midafternoon then, and the small room had not been empty. It had been almost full of humans and smaller animals—dogs on leads and cats in carrying boxes. One of the cats, Siamese by its voice, didn't want to be in a box, or at a place which smelled of other animals, and was mentioning it. When Siamese cats mention things they can be heard.

There were no other patients waiting to see the doctor this evening. The green fabric of the small sofa was just as morose as it had been a year—was it really a year?—before, when Colonel had walked in; been tugged in, actually. He, also, hadn't liked the smell of the place.

"I'll get something to put him on," Carol Arnold

17

said. "If you'll just ask Inspector Heimrich to bring him in, please. Doctor ought to be free any minute."

The pretty young woman went through a door, out of the waiting room. Susan went to the other door and beckoned to Merton, who began to extricate Colonel from the Buick. It was—as he had expected—going to be harder getting him out than it had been getting him in.

A tall young man wearing a summer sports jacket and red slacks walked from the large white house behind the hospital. He stopped by Heimrich.

"Big one, isn't he?" the young man said. "Give you a hand? Maybe go around the other side and give a push?"

"It'd help," Heimrich said.

The volunteer did help. They got Colonel out of the car, and Heimrich carried him to the hospital door. Susan stepped back from it to let them in. The young man came after them. And Carol Arnold came through the other door, dragging a pad. The helpful stranger moved, quickly, to aid her.

She said, "Hi, Lathe. I'm making out. You can just lay him down on it, Inspector."

Heimrich put Colonel down on the pad. Colonel was accepting.

"He's pretty old, isn't he?" Carol Arnold said. "It's beginning to show on his muzzle."

Colonel's muzzle was graying. Now, to both Susan and Merton Heimrich, it seemed grayer than it ever had before. He was pretty old.

"Inspector?" the man in the red slacks said.

"Yes. State Police, Mr.—?"

"Doctor, actually. Latham Rorke, M.D."

"Latham is a friend of mine," Carol said. "Now and then he just—drops by."

Rorke said, "Attagirl," for no reason apparent to either of the Heimrichs. He said, "Dropped by from White Plains, where I'm a lowly intern. With my one night a month off."

"One a fortnight," Carol said. "It could be Doctor went out the back way. Is at the house eating dinner. Only—"

"Only, I just came from there," Rorke said. "No Adrian. And Louise said to tell him dinner's ready. More than. And to tell you too, Carol. Unless—what about the Bird and Bottle?"

The conversation, to Susan and her husband, was scrappy. Casual, as between two who knew each other well, yet, Susan thought, with tension in it. The Bird and Bottle clarified things slightly. It was a restaurant a few miles away—a moderately celebrated restaurant.

Dr. Rorke said, "Yes?" to the pretty young woman. The Heimrichs might well have been somewhere else, somewhere a good distance off.

"I don't know," Carol Arnold said. "Louise has got dinner ready." She seemed suddenly to become conscious of the Heimrichs. "That's Mrs. Barton," Carol said. "I'm staying with them for the summer. You're sure he isn't at the house, Lathe?"

"If he is, Louise doesn't know it," Rorke said. "The Bird and Bottle, Carol child?"

"Maybe," the blond girl said. "After Doctor has looked at the dog. If he doesn't need me to help him. He ought to be out any minute now, Mrs. Heimrich. He's spaying one of Mrs. Cummins's cats, Lathe. It doesn't usually take him long. A Siamese named Jenny she's selling to somebody, I suppose. Somebody who doesn't want to breed. Just wants a pet." She looked at her watch. "But it is taking him a long time. I hope

19

there aren't complications. Particularly with a Linwood cat."

"You could knock on the door and ask him," Rorke said.

"When Adrian's operating, I'm not supposed to distract him. You know that, Lathe. Ought to, anyway."

"I like 'distract,'" Rorke said. "I like it very much."

There was, Susan thought, bite in his voice. It's nothing to do with us, she thought. Why doesn't this damn vet come out and do something about our dog? She looked down at Colonel. Anyway, he was still breathing. No thanks to Adrian Barton, DVM.

"Doctor ought to be out any minute, Mrs. Heimrich," Carol said. She did not seem to have heard Dr. Latham Rorke, or to have noticed the edge in his voice. "Anyway, he seems just to be sleeping, doesn't he?"

"He," Susan assumed, was Colonel. It could hardly refer to Dr. Barton. Or, conceivably, it could. Couldn't he hear voices from his operating room? Or did he choose not to?

"Yes," Susan said, "he does seem to be asleep. But, couldn't you ask the doctor when he'll be ready, Miss Arnold? After all, we've been waiting—well, quite a little time. If he could just look at Colonel and give us an idea? Whether he thinks there's anything he can do? If, of course, he's really finished with Mrs. Cummins's cat."

Carol Arnold said, "Well. He won't like it, but I suppose—"

She did not say what she supposed. Instead, she walked to a door at the end of the waiting room and knocked on it. She knocked tentatively. Then she said, "Doctor? Dr. Barton?"

She opened the door widely, and stopped and said, "Oh—oh, *no,*" her young voice rising. She almost screamed the *"no."*

The slender girl in white drew back from the opened door. She seemed to sway as she moved, but had regained balance by the time Rorke had taken long strides across the room and put his arms around her. But Rorke did not take his arms from around her.

From where he stood, Heimrich could see into the small, brightly lighted room. A fluorescent tube glared down on a small table. There was nothing on the operating table.

But on the floor beside the table a man was lying. He was rather a large man, but he looked crumpled as he lay on the floor. He wore a white jacket.

Heimrich could hear the girl's voice behind him as he went into the room.

"Not me, Lathe," Carol Arnold said. "Not *me—Adrian.* You're a doctor, aren't you? *Aren't* you, Lathe?"

2

DR. LATHAM RORKE knelt beside the crumpled man in the white jacket. He felt for a pulse; he turned Adrian Barton, DVM, on his back and leaned so he could listen to his chest. He straightened up and looked up at Heimrich.

"He'll have a stethoscope around," Rorke said. "In that little cabinet over there, probably. Next to the fridge."

Heimrich opened the cabinet Rorke had pointed at. The stethoscope was in it. He gave it to Rorke and Rorke listened through it. He listened at various points on the bared chest and, finally, sat back on his heels and again looked up at Heimrich. He took the stethoscope out of his ears.

"Nope," he said. "Looks like a DOA, Inspector." He got to his feet and looked at the girl, again in the doorway. "Sorry, Carol," he said. "I'm afraid Adrian's had it."

Carol Arnold said nothing. She put a hand up to her lips.

Heimrich had for some minutes been certain the big man on the floor was a dead man. He said, "Dead of what, Doctor?"

Rorke shrugged. He spread his hands in a gesture of defeat.

"Heart attack," Rorke said. "Fatal stroke, could be. And, I suppose, it could be diabetic coma. Take an autopsy to be certain. You see—"

"Dr. Barton was a diabetic, Doctor?"

"Told me so once," Rorke said. "Said it was mild but he was on insulin. On forty units a day. I wasn't his physician, you know. Chap named Chandler, I think his doctor was."

"And he forgot to take his insulin?" Heimrich said. "And went into coma and died in it. That's your guess, Doctor?"

"Only a guess," Rorke said. "A possibility. As I said, there'll have to be an autopsy to make sure. If Louise consents, I suppose."

"Even if she doesn't, I'm afraid. Dr. Chandler won't want to sign a certificate. And I don't know whether we could take it if he did. Would you think Dr. Barton would have been likely to forget his insulin shot, Doctor? After all, he was by way of being a medical man himself."

"No, I wouldn't. And they get so injecting it is automatic. And he did premed at Cornell. Required by their vet school, I understand. No, I'd think he'd be damn unlikely just to forget it. Half an hour before eating is the usual routine. Perhaps—" He stopped talking because Heimrich was not looking at him. Heimrich was looking down at the dead man. He was looking at a hypodermic syringe on the floor, partly hidden by a fold of Barton's white jacket, and near the flaccid right hand.

"Move him a little, Doctor," Heimrich said. "Toward you."

Rorke moved the body a little. They could both see the hypodermic then. Rorke reached a hand toward it.

"No, Doctor," Heimrich said. "I'll get it."

There was a box of Kleenex on the narrow counter under the cabinet next the small refrigerator. He took tissues out of it and used them to pick up the syringe. He wrapped the syringe carefully in tissues and put it in his pocket.

"For God's sake," Rorke said. "You act as if this were—I don't quite know how to put it. You—I guess it's as if you're acting like a cop."

"I am a cop," Heimrich said. "And we don't like sudden deaths. Particularly unexplained sudden deaths."

"Probably used the needle to shoot a barbiturate into the cat," Rorke said. "The one he was operating on. What they usually use for anesthesia."

"And, as they put it, to 'put animals to sleep,'" Heimrich said. "That is, to kill them. Something not allowed in your profession, of course."

"Not yet, anyway," Rorke said. "But already, I've seen cases where—"

He did not finish that. "Somebody'll have to tell Louise," he said.

Heimrich agreed. He said, "Miss Arnold?"

Carol Arnold was still in the doorway, Susan behind her. Heimrich had not spoken to Carol, but she answered—answered in a strangled voice. She said, "No. Please no, Inspector. I—I'm not up to it."

"You're damn right you're not," Rorke said. "I'll do it."

But then Carol said "No" again. "It's something

24

for me to do, isn't it? But, will you come with me, Lathe? In case—well, in case she needs something?"

Rorke looked at Heimrich and Heimrich nodded. "Yes," Heimrich said. "You'd both better go, I think. But, I'd like both of you to come back after you feel you can leave Mrs. Barton."

They did not leave the waiting room by the front door. They went, the girl ahead and Rorke very close behind her, by the doorway through which Carol had dragged the pad Colonel was sleeping on. Toward, presumably, the "back way" out.

"Look, dear," Susan said. "He's turned around. He's heading the other way."

It was quite true. At least, they both were sure it was true. Colonel's big head was at the opposite end of the pad from the end it had been. And, to both of them, he seemed to be breathing more easily.

"Could be it's just heat exhaustion," Heimrich said. "Maybe he's coming out of it. Cool in here, and could be he just needs rest where it's cool."

"Heat exhaustion? Like humans get?"

"They get most of the things we do, Susan. From head colds to cancer. We'll ask Miss Arnold about it when she gets back. Until then—well, Colonel will just have to wait."

Susan nodded. Murder, even possible murder, comes ahead of a dog, even a well-loved dog.

There was a telephone on the reception desk. Heimrick picked it up, but then put it down again. He found a Westchester–Putnam County telephone directory in the desk drawer. "Chandler Ernest MD ofc . . . Res. . . ." Ernest Chandler would be at home by now. Since it was Saturday, he had probably been at home all day. Or, of course, on the golf course of the Van Brunt Country Club. He dialed.

"Evening, Ernie," Heimrich said to their long-time family physician. "This is Heimrich."

Chandler, who does not like to be called "Ernie," retaliated. He said, "Hello, Merton." Heimrich does not like his given name. So they were now more or less even. In the friendliest possible fashion.

"This is more or less official," Heimrich said. "You had a patient named Barton? Dr. Adrian Barton. A vet?"

"Had?" Chandler said.

"I'm afraid so, Ernest. He's died. Rather suddenly."

"Suddenly enough to make you curious, apparently, M.L. Yes, he's been a patient of mine for the last couple of years."

"Diabetic, Doctor?"

Chandler hesitated, as Heimrich had known he would. Physicians do not discuss the ailments of their patients with outsiders.

"Barton's dead, Doctor," Heimrich said.

"Yes, diabetes. Fairly mild case."

"On insulin?"

"Of course. Forty units, before dinner. And a controlled carbohydrate intake. All balanced out. Hasn't had any problems lately, far's I know. And he'd have let me know if he'd had any. Not entirely a layman, you know."

"Had premed at Cornell, a doctor here tells me. An M.D., Ernest. A young one, interning in White Plains, he says. Name of Rorke. Latham Rorke. Ever hear of him?"

Dr. Chandler had never heard of Latham Rorke, M.D. Which meant nothing. "And, M.L.?"

"I'm at Dr. Barton's hospital," Heimrich said. "Rorke happened to be here. Confirmed death, actually. Not sure about the cause. Thinks diabetic coma is a possibility."

Chandler said, "Mmm."

Heimrich waited.

"People do die of it," Chandler said. "Not often, nowadays. Insulin brings them around. And other medications, of course."

"If Barton forgot his insulin injections, he might go into coma?"

"Not by missing one injection. And they don't forget them, M.L. Not if they're in their right minds. And Barton seemed to be in his right mind to me."

"But if he did forget? Both doses, say?"

"I wouldn't have thought so. Mild case, as I said."

"But it is possible?"

"M.L., I've been practicing medicine for a good many years. About thirty, actually. I've been at it too long to say that anything is impossible. Including voluntary remission of cancer. Had Barton been exercising violently during the afternoon?"

"I don't know. Would that make a difference?"

"It might."

"So far as I know, he was operating on a cat. Spaying a cat."

"For my money," Chandler said, "anything you try to do to a cat amounts to violent exercise. But probably it didn't for Barton. Treats a lot of cats, he told me once. Professional chitchat."

Which was, Heimrich thought, what this was in danger of turning out to be. "So you wouldn't," he said, "rule out the possibility of death in diabetic coma?"

"No," Chandler said. "Without examining the cadaver, I wouldn't rule out anything. But, I would think it entirely improbable. More likely cardiac arrest, although his EKG was all right a year or so ago. Pressure was up a little, way I remember it. Could have shot up in a year, of course. Does sometimes. Possibly a stroke, I suppose. However, I'm just guessing. With damn little to guess on."

Heimrich realized that, and thanked Ernest Chandler and hung up. Then he called the barracks and got things started. It was a suspicious death, which was enough to start with.

"I'm in the way," Susan said. "And, since there's no vet here to examine Colonel, I could take him home. Only he's too big to manage."

"Much too big," Heimrich said. "I'm afraid you'll just have to wait, dear. It may not be too long. The boys ought to be here before long. Maybe our doctor will say 'Natural causes' and we can both go home."

Susan went to the morose green sofa and sat on it. It was not only morose; it was hard. There were magazines on a table at one end of the sofa, but most of them seemed to be *Reader's Digests*. There was a copy of something called *The American Cat Fancy*. Susan decided to watch her dog.

"I'll have a look around while we wait," Heimrich said, and Susan responded with an "Mmm." Heimrich's look around started with a dead man.

Adrian Barton, DVM, had, at a guess, been in his middle or late forties. He had been almost startlingly handsome—tall and reasonably slender; dark-haired, firm-jawed. A strong, straight nose. Probably, Heimrich thought, attractive to women. Probably, although that was sheer guesswork, easily diverted by women. "Divert?" Why had that word come to mind? Yes, of course; Carol's word picked up by Latham Rorke with an edge in his voice. (Or was it "distract"?) He was, Heimrich thought, guessing ahead of himself.

Dark-haired, with no gray showing. Probably dark eyes. But that he could not tell, because the eyes were closed. A little unusual, that. Most die with their eyes open, as if they strained for a last glimpse of life.

Heimrich touched one of the outstretched arms. Yes, rigor had begun.

There were three doors in the small, narrow room. One opened on the waiting room, and Heimrich had just come through it. There was a door at either end of the room. Heimrich tried the one on his right.

It opened on a room with a desk in it and with filing cabinets. Dr. Barton's office. A door beyond the desk. The next room had a narrow table, similar to the operating table in the room Barton had died in. An arm of an X-ray machine was folded back against a wall, placed so it could be swung out over the table. There was a sterilizer, with instruments in it. All the instruments appeared to shine with cleanliness. A pair of surgical gloves, wrapped for sterility, lay at one end of the examining-operating table. There were cabinets on the wall, so set that the veterinarian could turn from the table and get what he needed out of any of them.

So, a well-equipped operating and examining room, for canine and feline patients.

Heimrich went back to the room with the body in it, and through the other door.

As he opened the door, a dog barked. Then another, louder dog barked. Then it seemed as if a dozen dogs barked, in mounting hysteria.

There were, actually, only six dogs in what was clearly the hospital's canine ward. They were of various breeds and sizes, and all, from a mammoth Newfoundland through a sizable golden retriever to a small smooth-haired fox terrier, making all the indignant noises they could manage. Indignant or, possibly, welcoming? Dogs expecting to be fed?

Beyond the dog ward, separated from it by a partly closed door, a quieter room, with cages along the wall, and cats in the cages—cats who, for the most part, were curled asleep on pads. The cages were roomy; each had its toilet pan with litter in it. Like the pan Mite used when he didn't want to go outdoors because it was cold outdoors. Or, of course, wet.

Most of the eight cats in the feline ward sat up when Heimrich went into their room. Several of them mewed at him, in a friendly fashion, but one large black tom hissed. One that sat up was a smallish sealpoint Siamese. Its posture and blue eyes were alert—too alert, he thought, for it to have just had surgery. There ought to be a relatively limp female along here somewhere. He looked in more cages.

He found the slender Siamese queen in a glass box near the far end of the room. There was a plaque above the glass box. It read, "No smoking! Oxygen." So. Postoperative patient in an intensive care ward, undergoing oxygen therapy.

The patient, another seal point, lay on her side. She had a bandage around her middle. She appeared to be soundly asleep and breathing easily. She flicked one brown, pointed ear as Heimrich looked down at her. He opened another door at this end of the ward.

The door opened on a narrow hallway, with a door at the end of and doors on either side. As Heimrich opened his door, the door at the far end of the hallway also opened. It was opened by a short, heavyset woman, probably somewhere in her sixties. Even from twenty feet away, she looked formidable. She was also wearing a man's felt hat. She wore a pants suit of dark gray and what Merton Heimrich's mother would have called "sensible" shoes.

She paid no attention to Heimrich. She said, "Roger? *Roger!*" She had a formidable voice. When she was not immediately answered, she took a step into the hall—a step which could easily be called a stride. And once more, she commanded somebody named Roger.

This time the door on the right side of the hall opened and a tall, rather gangling youth came through it. He had a book in one hand; he wore glasses. He had long blond hair, part of which dangled down his forehead. He pushed his hair back. He said, "Yes'm, Mrs. Cummins. Afraid I was reading."

"Jenny," the stocky woman said. "Ready?"

"Yes, Mrs. Cummins," Roger said. "Only she was still out, last I looked. Doctor said you'd be coming for her."

"I have," Mrs. Cummins said. "I'll get her."

Her voice was still inflexible. She started toward Heimrich, still in the doorway. She did not seem to see him, except as something in the way. He got out of it, and she strode past him into the animal wards.

"She likes to handle them herself, sir," Roger King said. Heimrich said "Evidently" to what was evident.

Mrs. Cummins was gone several minutes. Then she came back, a ventilated cat-carrying case in one hand. Heimrich again got out of her way. An indignant Siamese voice spoke from the black box.

"She's coming out of it, Mrs. Cummins," Roger said.

"Sounds like it," Mrs. Cummins said. "Let's hope she is, boy. That he didn't bungle this one. Two hun-

31

dred she's bringing, tabby markings or not. He give her the shots?"

"Yes'm. Said to tell you she's all set and he'd like you to keep an eye on her for a couple of days before they take her off."

Mrs. Cummins said, *"Huh,"* and went out the door with the carrying case. She went across smoothly mowed lawn to a blue Volks, parked partly on the grass. The boy pushed his drooping hair back again and said "Whew," more or less to himself. Then he said, "Sorry, sir. The doctor's probably up at the house."

"No, Roger, I'm afraid he isn't," Heimrich said. "He's still in the building. Only, he's dead, son. I'm Michael's father, Roger. Michael Faye. His stepfather, actually."

"Inspector Heimrich," the boy said. "You say Dr. Barton's dead, sir? *Jeez!*"

"Yes, Roger. They didn't tell you? Miss Arnold and Dr. Rorke, I mean. They went out this way a little while ago."

"No, nobody told me. I had my door closed, and maybe they didn't know I was here. I generally come in the back way. I was early this evening. You mean that's why you're here, Inspector? Because Dr. Barton's dead?"

"I brought a sick dog over," Heimrich said. "For the doctor to look at. It's because Dr. Barton's dead I'm still here. You work here, Roger?"

"Nights this summer," Roger said. "Sort of—oh, keep an eye on the animals. Go up and get the doctor at the house if—well, if I think one of them needs him. And feed them in the morning if the doctor's late. And change the cats' toilet pans. This time of year, the dogs can go out to the runs if they want to. I suppose I'm sort of a night watchman, sir. What happened to—I mean, what killed—the doctor?"

"We don't know yet, son. Possibly just heart failure. He seem all right to you when he spoke to you about Mrs. Cummins's cat? And when was that, Roger?"

"Six thirty, maybe. About then. Yes, he seemed just like always, I guess."

"That was after he had finished operating on the cat? Jenny? That's the cat's name, I take it. Pretty little cat."

"Mrs. Cummins is selling her, way I get it, sir. To some people who don't want to show her. Otherwise they wouldn't have her spayed, of course. Anyway, she was beginning to show tabby markings, so she'd be no good as a show cat. Mrs. Cummins has a cattery, you know."

Heimrich hadn't known; he'd begun to assume.

"Linwood, she calls it," Roger said. "Siamese mostly, according to Dr. Barton. He treats them when they need it. They are all fancy cats, Dr. Barton told me. I don't know much about the cat fancy, Inspector. What they call it. 'The fancy.'"

"More than I do," Heimrich told him. "About six thirty Dr. Barton came out and told you Mrs. Cummins's cat was ready for her to take home. He seemed to be all right then. Had you seen him earlier today?"

Roger King had not. He had himself come on duty at six, a few minutes earlier than usual. Usually, Miss Arnold stopped by his door and told him she was going up to the house. That he was in charge. Tonight she had not.

"Waiting for the doctor to finish operating, I suppose," Heimrich said. "So she could tell him Mrs. Heimrich and I were bringing Colonel over."

33

Roger didn't say, "Huh?" He merely looked it. "Colonel's the dog," Heimrich told him. "You can go back to your reading, son."

"Studying, really," the boy said. "Marine biology, sir. What I'm going in for, I think."

He carried his book into his room. Heimrich walked the length of the hallway and looked out the door. The Bartons' white house was about a hundred yards away. A big ash tree partly shaded it. There was no activity apparent in the house and no lights were on in it. Of course, dusk was only starting. Heimrich looked at his watch. Eight thirty. Make it eight thirty-two. Go up to the house and see how Mrs. Barton, newly widowed, was coming along? Not yet. Eventually, of course, if things developed so. Probably they wouldn't; probably Adrian Barton had been the victim of cardiac arrest and only that; probably Heimrich had been precipitate in his call to the barracks. On the other hand, the lab squad from Troop K was not being precipitate at all. Neither was the police doctor, nor the others who attend homicides. Well, probably there was no homicide to attend. Probably he ought to collect his wife, and their dog, and go home.

Probably analysis of what remained in the hypodermic syringe carefully tissue-wrapped in his pocket would turn out to be what was left of insulin, 40 U.

He closed the outside door, the back way out of the hospital and went back through the wards. The glass oxygen compartment was empty now; one of the caged cats was washing himself. No, herself. The black tom woke up long enough to hiss at Heimrich, but his heart didn't seem to be in it. The formerly alert seal-point Siamese lay with its creamy back to Heimrich and did not stir. In the canine ward, the dogs barked at him.

In the waiting room, Colonel was sitting up. He turned his head and looked at Heimrich. His eyes seemed even sadder than usual, and Heimrich thought there was a question in them. What are we doing in this place, which smells of hospital and of other animals? That probably was the question. Heimrich did not try to answer.

Susan, on the drab green sofa, was reading a small magazine. She put it down. "He seems to be much better," Susan said. "Perhaps it was a false alarm. Maybe we could take him home."

Heimrich shook his head.

"I called the barracks," he said. "I'll have to wait until the boys show up. Does he seem to be mobile?"

"Enough to sit up, anyway," Susan said. "About getting in the car, I don't know. You mean, if he can, I should drive him home and—well, get out from underfoot?"

It wasn't the way he would have put it. Heimrich's smile told her that.

"It'll be jammed up when they get here," he said. "Cops all over the place. Bodies being lugged around. One body, anyway. And I'll be hung up for a while. Not for too long, I hope. Probably a false alarm all around."

Susan stood and looked up at him. She looked for some seconds.

"You don't really believe it is, do you, dear?" she said. "I can tell, you know."

"Second sight, Susan?"

"Not second, Merton. Not even second thousandth. I've been looking at you for quite a while, Merton. So—say I've learned to see through you. You think Dr. Barton was murdered."

"I don't know, darling. But, well, I suppose I

think he could have been. Without anything really to go on."

"I'll see if Colonel is up to it," Susan said. "Otherwise you can carry him again, I suppose. But he'll have to get out on his own. He's too big for me to lug out at the other end."

"Much too big," Heimrich agreed. "If it comes to that, just leave him in the car. We'll have to find another vet."

"Yes," Susan said. "A live one." She walked toward the door. She said, "Come on, old fellow."

Colonel stood up. He seemed, Heimrich thought, faintly surprised that he could. But when he followed Susan to the door and out of it, he moved reasonably well. And when Heimrich opened the Buick's door, he hesitated only a minute. He did look around at Heimrich with what Heimrich thought was a "What, no help?" expression in his sad eyes. But he got into the car. He didn't bound in, but he got in. Come to think of it, he hadn't bounded in for some time. Colonel was getting to be an old, tired dog, past his bounding days.

3

AFTER SUSAN HAD DRIVEN the Buick away, Heimrich stood and looked at the white house. There was still no activity in the house. On the side he faced, which was the west side, closed venetian blinds obscured the windows. The last of the day's sun rays glittered on the windows.

There was a garage next to the south side of the house. The garage door was open, and there were two cars in the garage—a small black car and one much larger and also black. One of them Latham Rorke's? Probably. Dr. Rorke would hardly have walked up from White Plains.

Rorke and the pretty girl who was studying to be a veterinarian were certainly taking their time about it, it being telling a woman named Louise Barton that her husband was suddenly dead. Such things are not easy to tell, are best told gently. But how does one gentle such news, temper the harsh finality of such news? Heimrich himself had never found a way, although rather often the task had been his. Sorry, Mrs. Barton. Bad news, I'm afraid. The husband you were expecting home for dinner won't be coming. He's lying dead on the floor of his operating room. Not much good. What is good?

Perhaps Carol and the young man who had driven up hoping to take her to dinner had decided to eat the dinner Louise Barton had prepared for her husband. And for Carol? Apparently Carol was living in the Barton house. For the summer, anyway. Before she went back to Ithaca and the study of animal ailments. Odd profession for a very pretty young woman to choose.

Heimrich had taken a few steps toward the hospital when he heard a car coming up Barton Lane. The boys from the barracks, probably. Or the ambulance, complete with medical examiner, from Cold Harbor.

The car was a very red Volks. It went to the house and stopped in front of it, and a woman got out. She was small and compact and, from her movements, middle-aged. Middle-aged and a little arthritic. But she moved quickly to the front door of the big white house and opened the door—without, so far as Heimrich could tell, ringing the doorbell. She went into the house. So, reinforcement for the bereaved.

Heimrich went on to, and into, the small animal hospital.

Nothing had changed there, except that Barton's body presumably had stiffened further. And where the hell were Heimrich's own reinforcements? If they hadn't moved the Troop K barracks so far to the north, they would have arrived by now. And Cold Harbor was much closer. In a heat wave, everything slows down.

He went through the animal wards. The dogs

barked at him. The black cat was asleep and didn't wake up to hiss. The door of Roger King's room was closed and Roger was typing behind it. A diligent student, apparently. Or, for all Heimrich knew, a boy typing a love letter to a girl. A boy not much interested in sudden death.

Heimrich opened the back door and stood in the doorway and looked at the white house. He was just in time. Carol Arnold and Rorke were just coming out the door. They were coming out merged, Rorke's right arm firmly around the girl.

Not, Heimrich was reasonably sure, to support her, or for purposes of consolation. Well, they were a handsome young couple and Rorke had driven some miles from White Plains on a hot, humid evening, in the hope that he might take her to dinner. And there had been sharpness, almost animosity, in his voice when he spoke of Adrian Barton. So. And Rorke was a doctor. And he had known, or very accurately guessed, where Rorke kept his stethoscope. Mmm.

And Barton probably had died of cardiac arrest. Or, conceivably, in diabetic coma, whatever Ernest Chandler thought probable.

Carol and Latham Rorke saw him standing in the doorway as they walked toward the hospital. For half the distance, Rorke kept his arm around the girl. Then, very slowly, he removed it. The lingering removal was like a caress.

"Sorry we were so long, Inspector," Carol said when they were only a few yards away. "We were waiting for Louise's sister to come and be with her. It —it was an awful shock to Louise, of course. Lathe gave her a sedative, and we called her doctor and Mary."

Who was, presumably, the sister.

"You did want to talk to me about it, didn't you, Inspector? About what happened to Adrian. Because —well, you act as if you don't think it was a natural death. Is that it?"

"When an apparently healthy man dies suddenly, without medical attendance, we always wonder a little, Miss Arnold. It's a matter of routine."

"Adrian wasn't entirely healthy," the girl said. "He had diabetes. Didn't Lathe tell you that?"

Rorke had. And Barton's own doctor had confirmed it. And termed it mild. And, yes, Heimrich did want to have a few words with Miss Arnold about the events of the afternoon. For example—

Heimrich did not get to his example. Cars arrived at the animal hospital. Tires scraped on gravel as wheels were braked. If Miss Arnold would wait for a while; probably not too considerable a while. Just until things became a little clearer. If she and Dr. Rorke wanted to go to dinner, it would be all right. As long as they were not too long about it.

"Louise had dinner ready," Carol said. "But—it didn't seem right to eat there. With poor Louise—"

Funeral baked meats, Heimrich thought. Although that wasn't, of course, entirely accurate. But, he told them, he understood entirely.

"Not the Bird and Bottle, I guess," Rorke said. "Not a place to eat and run, exactly. The Tavern, Carol?"

There was a restaurant in Cold Harbor called the Tavern. It wasn't, by a long stretch, the Bird and Bottle, but it was near.

"All right," Carol said, and the two of them walked toward the white house and, presumably, the garage adjacent to it. After they had taken a few steps, Rorke put an arm about the girl again. She had changed out of her white uniform into a sleeveless pale green dress.

Heimrich did not wait until they reached the garage. He went to the front door of the hospital to greet his reinforcements.

They were numerous—Lieutenant Charles Forniss in one car and Corporal Purvis, in uniform, with him; the lab truck from the barracks; an ambulance from the Cold Harbor hospital. And, from the last car in line, a man with a black bag getting out. Forniss said, "Evening, M.L." Purvis said, "Sir," and saluted. Dr. James Marvin said, "Got a dead one, Inspector? Hot night for it."

Heimrich agreed he had a dead one and added that, from the police point of view, it might be a false alarm. Marvin said, "Huh? Not shot? Not knifed? No blunt instrument?"

"Just suddenly dead," Heimrich said. "The vet who runs this place, Doctor. Dr.—"

"Ad Barton," Marvin said, and added that he'd be damned. "Hell," he said, "Adrian and Louise were coming to our place for Sunday lunch tomorrow. Unless he had a dying dog or something. Or I had an emergency. Where is he?"

Apparently Marvin and Barton had been friends. Barton was still "he" to James Marvin, M.D. To medical examiners, cadavers quickly become "it."

Heimrich took Dr. Marvin to Barton's body, stiffening on the floor of his operating room.

"Dead a couple of hours," Marvin said. "Rigor's setting in. Just fell down dead, you think? Where he is now?"

"Apparently," Heimrich said. "Oh, we moved him a little. This was partly under him."

He took the wrapped syringe out of his pocket.

41

He said, "Hold it just a minute, Doctor. Better have this printed."

Forniss had come in with them. Heimrich handed the tissued syringe to Lieutenant Forniss, who said, "Yep," and carried it out toward the lab truck.

Marvin knelt beside the corpse. He pushed back the closed eyelids, and closed them again.

"Just dead," Marvin said. "Have to open him up to find out why. Could be a heart attack, from the looks of it. You closed his eyes, Inspector?"

"No. Closed when we found him."

"We?"

"A young doctor from White Plains. Had come up to take his girl to dinner. Name of Rorke. Ever hear of him, Doctor?"

"Barton mentioned him once, I think. Said he was badgering Carol. Pretty kid, she is. Kind anyone would be likely to make passes at."

"Yes," Heimrich said. "Barton used the word 'badgered'?"

"Way I remember it," Marvin said. "You want to take pictures of it before we take it away?"

Heimrich did want pictures taken. Forniss came back. The hypodermic syringe was now unwrapped. "One set," Forniss said. "Where you'd expect them to be."

"Probably Barton's," Heimrich said. "Better print him before they take him away."

"They're coming," Forniss said.

Heimrich gave the syringe to Dr. Marvin.

"Empty," Marvin said. "On the floor beside him, you say?"

"As if he'd dropped it as he fell, Doctor."

"Adrian was a diabetic," Marvin said. "Mild case. Apparently under control. Insulin."

"Yes," Heimrich said. "Dr. Chandler told me that."

"Good old Ernie," Marvin said. "Still practicing. When I get to be his age, I hope I'm retired. Not that he isn't a damn good man. So he was treating Adrian, was he? Mild case, way Adrian thought?"

"Yes, Doctor."

"Probably forty units, then," Marvin said. "Maybe before breakfast—blood glucose highest in the morning—or in the evening, half an hour or so before dinner. But injecting the stuff is a bit of a nuisance, even when you've got used to it. What time would he be having dinner, do you know?"

Heimrich didn't. Probably Miss Arnold would know. Apparently she had her meals with the Bartons. When they had found Barton's body, his dinner had been ready and waiting. Mrs. Barton had sent word to that effect, by Rorke.

"Times fit," Marvin said. "What your lab boys will find a residue of in this syringe will be insulin, hundred to one."

"He'd operated on a cat just before he died," Heimrich said. "Don't vets anesthetize animals by injection?"

"Barbiturates," Marvin said. "Dosage by weight of animal. So, nowadays, do we. Sodium pentothal, usually. For starters. You think maybe he injected himself instead of the cat? Not likely, Inspector. Not with the same needle, obviously. Thousand to one, your boys will find insulin was in this syringe. Maybe with zinc, more likely regular. You're thinking of insulin shock?"

"Just wondering about the whole thing," Heimrich told him.

"Have to take a good many times the normal

dose," Marvin said. "Not likely to. They get so measuring the prescribed dosage is pretty automatic. One c.c., usually. Forty units of insulin per one c.c. Marked on the syringe. See?"

Heimrich looked at the cylinder of the hypodermic. It was marked in cubic centimeters.

"Also," Marvin said, "he'd be using the needle on a lot of animals. All sorts of medications by injection. Animals don't like to take pills. Particularly cats, I gather."

Marvin was damned right. Heimrich told him so with feeling. He had had, a year or so before, to give Mite pills. It had been arduous, although in the end successful. When the pills finally got into Mite they were accompanied by blood from human fingers. Cats do not approve of taking pills.

"Are there poisons of which one c.c., by needle, would be lethal, Doctor?"

"Sure. Dozens, possibly. You're thinking maybe he got the stuff out of the wrong vial? Inspector, Adrian was a pro. Going to be damn sure what he shoots into himself. However, anything he might have used by accident would be in his refrigerator there. We can look."

They looked into the small refrigerator set into the wall. There were a number of bottles and vials in it. They were arranged in racks.

"There's his insulin," Marvin said. He pointed to the racked small vials. All but one had red caps on them. The little vials were labeled, "Lilly, Iletin (R) 40 U. Regular." They were also marked, "10 cc."

The one vial without a red aluminum cap had a stopper in it.

"One he was using," Marvin said. "Rubber plug, see? Special kind of rubber. You push the needle through it and get out what you want. Pull the needle out and the rubber seals itself."

He held the vial up to the light and looked at it.

"About four c.c.'s left, at a guess," Dr. Marvin said.

He put the little vial back in its appointed place in the rack. He looked at, without touching, the other small bottles and vials in the refrigerator.

"Pretty much what you'd expect," Marvin said. "Barbiturates in solution. Sodium pentothal, of course. Knocks them out in seconds. Out for good, if that's what's wanted. A good many things we don't use on human patients. A few've been tried and didn't work. Or worked too damn well, sometimes. Where are these photographers of yours, if you're still going to treat it as homicide?"

"Waiting for us to get out of the way," Heimrich told him.

They got out of the way into the waiting room.

The police photographer went into the narrow operating room, and the bulbs flashed. The photographer came out and the fingerprint men began dusting, and lifting prints and taking pictures of what they found.

Dr. Marvin looked at his watch. He said, "No point in my sticking around that I can see. Autopsy report'll be along in the morning sometime."

"And lab findings," Heimrich said.

"If I can get the lab boys on it," Marvin told him. "After all, it's a weekend, Inspector."

Heimrich knew it was a weekend. He also knew that hospitals run short-staffed on weekends. (And that Sunday was supposed to be his own day off. It was a tattered supposition.)

He said, "When you can, Doctor."

Dr. Marvin flipped a hand in a gesture which might mean anything. He went out toward his car. Heimrich continued to wait. It was twenty minutes, it was almost nine thirty, before the fingerprint men came out of the office. One of them said, "All through, sir. Way it looks, the prints on the syringe are his, all right. Same type, anyway. We'll check them out and send the report along. Monday be all right?"

Heimrich supposed it would have to be. He also supposed there would be a good many prints in the operating room and that not all of them would be those of Adrian Barton, DVM. To that, the fingerprint man said, "Sure are, sir."

Forniss had been outside, looking around. He came in as the fingerprint men went out. He said, "Tell them to come and get it, M.L.? They want the ambulance for live ones."

Heimrich said, "Yes, Charles."

One of the fingerprint men said, "Want we should tell them, Inspector?"

Heimrich said "Yes" again. He and Forniss sat on the green sofa.

Forniss said, "Onto something, M.L.?"

"Doesn't look much like it," Heimrich said. "Find anything outside, Charley?"

Forniss had not. After the blacktop of Barton Lane ended, there was only gravel, loose gravel. Cars had roughed it up without leaving behind any tire marks. Oh, there was one thing. "Around back somebody drove up on the grass. Light car, looks like. Maybe a Volks."

"Yes," Heimrich said. "A Mrs. Cummins. Came to pick up her cat."

"So?" Purvis said. "We just wait for reports."

That was about it, Heimrich told him—for reports that probably would show that Barton had died

46

of heart failure; that the residue in the syringe would be residue of insulin, 40 U, with which Dr. Barton had injected himself half an hour before dinnertime. Or, of course, thereabouts.

"There's a girl works here," Heimrich said, "Studying to be a vet, and getting practical experience during vacation. Very pretty girl named Carol—Carol Arnold. The kind, Dr. Marvin says, any man might make a pass at. Man named Rorke's probably making a pass at her now. Several passes, from the time they're taking over dinner at the Tavern."

"The one in Cold Harbor?" Forniss said. "Hamburger and pizza joint, mostly. Shouldn't take them long. She know you want to talk to her, M.L.?"

"I asked her to come back, Charley. She was here this afternoon. Almost certainly when Barton died. She'd been told not to disturb him, because he was operating on a cat."

Forniss merely raised inquiring eyebrows.

"Nothing," Heimrich said. "Just what went on during the afternoon. If she has a record of who brought animals in for treatment. If anything unusual happened. Whether pet owners were allowed inside Barton's examining room. That sort of thing. Probably all a waste of time, because Barton probably—just died."

"Unaided, you mean?"

"Unaided, Charley. And a nosy cop just happened to be here. As a pet owner, Charley."

He told Forniss about Colonel. Forniss offered sympathy. He said old Colonel was quite a dog, and was agreed with. And so they just waited the return of Carol Arnold and a man named Rorke?

"A doctor," Heimrich said. "Also, apparently, a boy friend. Yes."

But then he stood up. "Could be," he said,

"they've already come back and gone up to the house instead of coming here. Suppose I go see, Charley. If they show up, you can go to the back door and semaphore or something. You can semaphore?"

"Sure," Forniss, who is an ex-marine, told his longtime superior and longtime friend.

"Good," Heimrich said. "Not that I can read it, of course."

Inspector Heimrich went out the back door and across the smooth lawn toward the white house.

4

ONLY THE LARGER of the black cars was in the garage. Which meant, presumably, that Carol and Latham Rorke were still ingesting pizza, or hamburgers, at the Tavern. Or were doing something else, not necessarily at the Tavern. Which reminded Merton Heimrich that he had not had dinner, although it was getting on for ten. He hoped that Colonel had got out of the Buick under his own power and that Susan had eaten dinner, not waited fruitlessly for him.

He went to the white house. He could express sympathy and regret to Louise Barton, who would know from Carol Arnold that there was a policeman bumbling around. Needlessly and to no result. He rang the doorbell. The door was opened almost at once by the compact, middle-aged woman he had seen going into the house earlier. The sister, presumably. Mary Something. Heimrich told her who he was and that he would like to see Mrs. Barton, if she was up to it.

"I don't think she is," the sister said. "Isn't it enough that her husband's dead? And that the police are messing around? Though why I don't know."

"Sudden death, with no physician there," Heimrich said. "Sort of thing we always have to look into, Miss—"

"Mrs. Mrs. Evans."

"Mrs. Evans. It's the law."

"Well, she's lying down. That young doctor gave her something. My sister's terribly upset, Inspector. Who wouldn't be?"

Heimrich agreed that anyone would be upset. He would like a few words with Mrs. Barton. He would try not to upset her further.

Well, Mary Evans supposed so. She couldn't see why, but she supposed so.

Louise Barton was lying on a sofa in the living room of the big house. The sofa was very large and the woman on it was very small. She was short and thin. Distressingly thin, and gray-haired. She appeared to be older than the strong, handsome man Heimrich had looked down on on the operating-room floor.

Mrs. Barton's eyes were closed when Mary Evans led Heimrich into the room. She opened them and looked up at the tall police inspector. She closed them again.

"A policeman, dear," Mrs. Evans said. "An Inspector something. Do you feel up to talking to him, Lou?"

Louise Barton moved her head from side to side. She did not open her eyes. "You see?" Mary Evans said. "It's like I told you. That young man who was with Carol gave her something. Said he was a doctor, she told me. I've called Dr. Reynolds, but it always takes him forever. If he comes at all."

"Dr. Rorke probably gave her a sedative," Heimrich said. "That right, Mrs. Barton?"

She turned her head toward him. She opened her eyes. She said, "There's no need to shout, whoever you are."

Heimrich had not shouted. He said again who he was, and spoke in a lowered voice.

"What he said it was," Louise Barton said. "Said it would relax me. Make things easier for me. But my husband's dead, Inspector. *Dead!*"

"Yes, Mrs. Barton, I'm afraid he is. Did he have any trouble with his heart, do you know?"

"Never. He was always so healthy. For all he was older. Than I am, I mean. And vigorous always. He played tennis whenever he got a chance. We'd talked about having a court put in. Oh. And now—*now.*"

"You see," Mary Evans said, "you *are* upsetting her. I'll make him go away, Lou. Quit bothering you."

"It's all right, Mary," Louise said. "Probably he thinks he has to. What made him die, Inspector? He was all right at lunch. He seemed just fine. And we were very careful about his diet always. The one Dr. Chandler put him on. No sugar, of course. And very few of any other carbohydrates."

"Yes," Heimrich said. "I heard Dr. Barton was diabetic, Mrs. Barton. He always had his meals here? I mean, came here from the hospital for lunch and dinner?"

"Of course." She swung around to a sitting position on the sofa. Her eyes now were very wide open, staringly open. "You think I *poisoned* him? Poisoned Adrian?"

"Of course not," Heimrich said. "Why should I think a thing like that? Just lie back and rest, Mrs.

51

Barton; try to, anyway. I know how you must be feeling."

She said, "How can you?" but she lay back on the sofa. She closed her eyes again. She said, "I don't know whether you're married, Inspector. But suppose it was your wife. All at once dead. And people poking around about it?"

"I am married, Mrs. Barton. And I'd find it very —hard." "Hard" wasn't adequate; Heimrich felt the entire inadequacy of "hard." If Susan—

"Hard," Louise said. "You'd find it *hard!*"

"I'm sorry," Heimrich said. "Very sorry. I'm afraid I am upsetting you, as your sister says."

She turned on her side, away from him. When she spoke, her voice was so low he could hardly hear her.

"I had dinner all ready," she said. "At seven, like always. I asked that girl—no, it was that young man, her friend—to tell him dinner was ready. He was late, you see. He's almost never late."

Again, Heimrich said he was sorry he had had to bother her. He moved toward the door, and Mary Evans moved after him. Almost, he thought, as if she were a rear guard, vigilant against his return.

At the door, she said, "I knew you'd upset her. And I can't see what good it did you. Adrian's just as dead as ever, and that's all she cares about."

Heimrich didn't see, either, that talking to Mrs. Barton had done him any good. But—

"When your sister said 'that girl,' " he said. "I suppose she meant Miss Arnold?"

"Of course."

"Do you happen to know whether Miss Arnold has been living here with the Bartons, Mrs. Evans? Having her meals with them?"

"Yes. Since June, I think. She's been working

with the doctor. She's going to be a vet, according to what she told them. Studying to be, she says. Funny thing for a girl to want to be, seems to me. Messing around with animals."

"Yes," Heimrich said. "Vets have to do that. Go back and be with your sister, Mrs. Evans."

"Not supposed to call them 'vets,' " she said. "They don't like it. Only that's what they call each other. Last summer it was a boy."

Heimrich said, "Sorry?"

"Who came here to work with Adrian. To get practical experience, they call it. Nice enough boy, from what I saw."

"Well," Heimrich said, "thank you, Mrs. Evans. And I'm sorry to have to bother you both at a time like this."

It was not much of an exit line, but exit was indicated. Also, Forniss was standing at the back door of the hospital, looking toward the house. He was not making semaphore gestures. He was merely beckoning.

Heimrich crossed the lawn again. Forniss said, "Yep. They've showed up, M.L."

Roger King was still typing when they went past his room off the hallway. If it was a letter to his girl, it was a long one. Rorke and Carol Arnold were side by side on the sofa. They were not especially close together. Deliberately not? Heimrich wondered.

He was sorry if he'd kept them waiting. He wouldn't be long. He just wanted to ask Miss Arnold a few things about the afternoon. He wouldn't need to keep Dr. Rorke.

"If you want me to clear out?" Rorke said. "Evening's shot anyway. That Tavern place you sent us to isn't so hot, Inspector."

Heimrich said he was sorry about that. It was an evening he seemed to be sorry about a good many things, starting with Colonel's apparent need for medical attention. And Dr. Rorke could stay around if he wanted to. His questions to Miss Arnold would be few and routine.

Rorke looked at the girl beside him. Neither of them said anything. Rorke looked from the girl to Heimrich. "Then I guess I'll stick around," he said.

Heimrich nodded. He said, "About this afternoon, Miss Arnold. Anything out of the way happen? Until we found Dr. Barton, of course."

"Just like most afternoons," she said. She had a low-pitched voice, a soft voice. "A lot of dogs and cats. And people too, of course. One dog had been hit by a car, and Ad—Dr. Barton took him first. Jaw all smashed up, the poor little tike. Dr. Barton fixed him up. The owner took him home, although the doctor wanted to keep him overnight. The rest were—oh, shots, mostly. Rabies shots. Things like that. Distemper shots. Enteritis shots for the cats. And a cat with, Dr. Barton thought, perhaps viral pneumonia. Only it could be lung congestion, which they get sometimes. That one I held while the doctor gave him the anesthetic so he could X-ray him. There wasn't any congestion."

A good deal about the animals; not very much about the people. He supposed she had a list of the people?

"Of course. And the names of the animals. One of the dogs was actually named Rover, believe it or not. Do you want the list, Inspector?"

"No," Heimrich said. "Not now, anyway. Did any of the people who brought animals in go into the examining rooms, do you remember?"

"Some did. Some owners want to hold their pets

while the doctor treats them. People with cats, mostly. Somebody has to hold them, you know. Usually it's me, but some cat people—well, they don't want to trust anybody. Dr. Barton treats—treated—a lot of cats."

"Just small animals? I mean the animals Dr. Barton treated?"

Heimrich had difficulty determining why he had asked that. He was already getting a good deal of information he didn't particularly want. If, indeed, it turned out he wanted any information at all about Dr. Adrian Barton's sudden death.

"He treated horses and cows when he first came here, I think. Recently, it's been just small animals. They can't bring horses and cows in, you know. Or sheep. Not that there are many sheep around here. When I get my license, I plan to go in for horses mostly, I think. General practice, anyway."

"You're not big enough for horses, baby," Rorke said. "They'll push you around."

"I like horses, Lathe," the girl said. "Also, they don't scratch."

"No," Rorke said. "Just trample."

They'd much rather talk to each other than to me, Heimrich thought. Now and then I find myself calling Susan "baby." So.

"Just a routine afternoon, then," he said. "No different from the ones you usually have here. How long have you been working with Dr. Barton, Miss Arnold?"

"Since early June. When the term was over."

"And you probably got to know him fairly well since you've been here."

"We got along all right. He was an easy man to work with."

Rorke turned and looked at her. Then he looked

away again, but this time not at Heimrich. The way they were seated, Heimrich could not see the expression on the young man's face.

"Ever ask you to play tennis with him, Miss Arnold? His wife says he played every chance he got. And, well, she doesn't really look like a tennis player."

"She was until a few years ago, Inspector. What he told me, anyway. Yes, I played with him a couple of times. Didn't give him much of a game. He was a lot too good for me. Way out of my class."

More information which applied to nothing.

"About when did Dr. Barton go to operate on Mrs. Cummins's cat, Miss Arnold?"

"Around six. Mrs. Cummins had brought her in a little after four. Wanted her operated on right then. But the doctor was working on the little dog with the smashed jaw. It was an emergency, of course. Mrs. Cummins was a little annoyed. She doesn't think much of dogs. People are funny, Inspector."

Heimrich's smile and nod agreed with the girl's generalization.

"So, she left the cat? The one she's selling. The one they call Jenny?"

"Took her out to the cages," Carol said. "Wanted to do it herself. Pick the right cage, I guess. She knows her way around here pretty well. Adrian took care of all her cats. We still have another seal point of hers here. Mrs. Cummins's a breeder, you know. We gave them their enteritis shots, that sort of thing."

"And neutered them, apparently?"

"Not often. They're show cats, Inspector. Show cats aren't spayed or castrated, you know."

Heimrich hadn't. He nodded his head again, this time to show he had.

"About six, Dr. Barton went out to get Jenny to operate on her."

"About then."

"And about half an hour after that, my wife called about our dog and you told her the doctor could have a look at him in about half an hour. That's right? It took him about an hour to do the operation?"

"It varies. Some of them resist the anesthetic. Sometimes there are complications. I—well, I allowed plenty of time. Thought I did. It was after you and Mrs. Heimrich brought the Dane in that I thought—well, that it was taking him longer than usual. And—"

"Yes, Miss Arnold. How did you happen to come here, by the way?"

"I wrote and applied," she said. "For several years, Dr. Barton has been having students from the school come down in the summers. To get practical experience. The dean thinks it's a good idea. A boy who was here last year told me about it, so I wrote the doctor. And he—I suppose he checked me out. At the school, I mean. Anyway, he said to come down and we'd talk it over. So, I came down and we worked things out. Not that there was much to work out. I was to live with them, Dr. and Mrs. Barton and—well, watch and help out when I could. As I said, a sort of internship. Dean Smedley was all for it. Dr. Barton was a Cornell man himself, you know. He came up for guest lectures now and then."

Heimrich said he saw. "And you've found Dr. Barton an easy man to work with?"

She said, "Oh, yes."

Latham Rorke appeared to have withdrawn. He was looking at the wall opposite. He seemed to be looking at it rather fixedly. It was, Heimrich thought, as if he wanted to make his detachment evident. Disapproving? Perhaps even jealous? With cause for jealousy?

A detective gets involved with things which do

not concern him; things which are no business of his. This happens in all cases. It can even happen when, as now, there is not really a case.

Merton Heimrich stood up. Forniss, who had been sitting at the other end of the room and been reading a magazine, stood too. He put the small magazine—how small most magazines had got in recent years!—into his jacket pocket. A magazine he had brought with him, apparently.

They went out to the police car. "Sent young Purvis back with the lab boys," Forniss said. "Didn't figure you'd need him."

"No," Heimrich said. "I'm not too sure we need anybody."

"Want to stop somewhere for a sandwich, M.L.?"

Heimrich did not. Forniss drove him home. No, he guessed he wouldn't come in for a drink.

He had started the engine and was shifting into drive when he took the small magazine out of his pocket. He held it out to Heimrich. "Afraid I walked off with this," he said. "Maybe you'll want to take it back, if you go to the hospital again. Or I can go around and put it back, on my way to the barracks. I've got the duty tonight."

Heimrich doubted he would be going back to the small animal hospital of the late Adrian Barton, DVM. But he took the magazine. It had a simple title. The title was *The American Cat Fancy*. Only inside was the title amplified. It became "The Fanciers Journal." At the foot of the Contents page, "Published monthly" caught his eye, and a Philadelphia address.

5

THE BUICK WAS IN THE GARAGE. Colonel was not in the
Buick. Which was something of a relief.

It was cool in the long, low house. Usually, they
could turn the air conditioner off after sunset, even in
weather as hot as this. But now it was still running.
Of course, for Colonel's benefit. Susan had, he
guessed, diagnosed heat exhaustion.

Colonel was lying, on his side and in apparent
comfort, in front of the fireplace, with summer logs
stacked neatly in it. Mite was lying, also extended,
between Colonel's forepaws. Animals get habit fixa-
tions. If it is a sound idea to lie in front of a fire in cold
weather, it remains a good idea to lie in front of the
same fireplace in summer.

Colonel lifted his big head and looked at Heimrich. He did not say anything, but he has never been
a talkative dog. Susan said "Hi" from the kitchen.
"Have you had anything to eat?" Merton had not, and
said he hoped she had.

"A sandwich," Susan said and came out of the kitchen. "Toasted cheese be all right? Or cold cuts, only the beef is well done. Gray done. And shall we have our other drink, or is it too late for a martini?"

She looked at the animals in front of the nonfire.

"He got out of the car all right," she said. "I wouldn't say with alacrity, but he got out. And he ate dinner. Part of it, anyway. And he doesn't smell sick to Mite, obviously. Sometimes other animals seem to be able to tell better than vets. Speaking of vets?"

Heimrich sat down and stretched his legs out. He also sat in front of the fireplace. An animal doesn't have to have four legs to become fixated. Susan stood and looked at him. Then she said she'd get the ice and turned back toward the kitchen. Heimrich raised his voice a little to answer her question. His answer was they didn't know yet. He heard ice rattle into the glass mixer. He waited until Susan came back, carrying a tray with bottles on it, and the ice-filled mixing glass, and the properly chilled stemmed glasses. And, of course, the lemon and the bar knife. It was after ten, and a hell of a time for before-dinner drinks.

"Probably natural causes," Merton said, as he mixed drinks on the table between their chairs. "Probably a lot of fuss about nothing. Starting because Colonel's an old dog and got to feeling the heat. The lab boys are on it, and the pathologist at Cold Harbor. Probably his heart just stopped. They do, sometimes."

They clicked glasses and sipped. Susan looked at their animals, basking in the heat that wasn't. Then she turned to Merton Heimrich and for several seconds looked at him without speaking.

"Only," Susan Heimrich said, "you don't think so, do you? This man York, you think?"

"Rorke," Heimrich said. "Latham Rorke, M.D. I don't know what I think, dear. Nothing to go on."

She continued to look at him, her lips in a patient smile.

"All right," Heimrich said. "A policeman is always curious and usually suspicious. As enjoined to be in the textbooks. Why Rorke, Susan?"

"Jealous," Susan said. "In love with the pretty girl. Thinks she and the vet were playing around. Whether or not they were, it would be what *he* thought, wouldn't it?"

Heimrich said, "Intuition, dear?"

"Observation," Susan said.

"And you think Carol and Dr. Barton were lovers?"

"Merton, dear," Susan said, "however would I know? I never saw them together. When they were both alive, that is."

She finished her drink and stood up. "I'll do your sandwich," she said. "While you have another."

She went back to the kitchen. Heimrich made himself another drink.

The implication was, he thought, that had Susan seen Barton and Carol Arnold together, and both alive, Susan would have known whether they were lovers. Well, he thought, she probably would have. And so, possibly not quite so quickly, would I. Lovers give themselves away. Even if they are sitting across a room from each other. He looked toward the kitchen as he finished his drink.

Of course, if Rorke had noticed, or thought he noticed, intimacy between Carol and her employer—for room and board, apparently—others might have noticed too. Mrs. Barton? She certainly would have had opportunity. To observe small movements, to hear intonations in voices. Assuming she was an observant woman.

She would, almost certainly, know her way

around the hospital. Better than Latham Rorke, M.D., who clearly knew his rather well. Almost as well as Carol Arnold had, in a couple of months, learned to know her way. If, say, she had loved Barton and been dropped by her lover? That certainly came within police experience, as it had in that of Oscar Wilde. Who had, perhaps, extended it beyond acceptance. But Wilde had been a poet.

Heimrich was not. He was a cop waiting for his wife to bring him a toasted cheese sandwich. And for the telephone to ring, being fairly sure it wouldn't, at least for hours. Things move slowly on summer weekends, even in hospitals and police labs.

He leaned down and rubbed Colonel behind the ears. Colonel sighed a contented sigh. "You got us into something, old boy," Heimrich told his dog. Colonel opened his eyes. They were sad, as they were always sad. But there was response in them.

Then Colonel got up. He was no more laborious about it than usual—than, Heimrich realized, he had been about it for some months; perhaps for as much as a year. Age brings its changes slowly; one is apt to take them for granted. Except, of course, as regards oneself.

Mite, bereft, arched his back. Then he jumped to Heimrich's lap, circled and curled. He also purred. Heimrich scratched behind Mite's ears, and Mite made sounds of appreciation.

Susan brought the sandwich. She had toasted bacon in it. After Heimrich had eaten it, and after Colonel had returned from the kitchen, they had mild Scotches and water. After all, it was Saturday night. Sunday was Merton's day off, as befitted inspectorship. And *susan faye fabrics* was never open on Sundays. It was not, for that matter, open in July, although Susan often went to the shop on Van Brunt Avenue to do designs in the back room.

They sat silently. Mite, who had not got any of Heimrich's sandwich, although not for want of trying, went off after his dog. When they had finished their drinks, Susan and Merton Heimrich went to bed.

The telephone did not ring. It had not rung at a little before midnight, when Merton left Susan's bed and occupied his own. It had not rung at a little after seven, when the summer sun awakened them both. The sun was assisted by Colonel, who woofed his readiness for breakfast, and to go out. Mite, as usual, let the big dog speak for both of them. Mite does not waste meows.

Susan and Merton had breakfast on the terrace. Distant church bells softly summoned them to mass at Saint Mary's. They did not respond to the gentle suggestion. "Poor Father Maloney," Susan said. "I hope some of his flock—well, flocks."

Heimrich said "Mmm." He noted that this was Presbyterian country, Episcopalian in the higher echelons.

"And we're heathens," Susan said. "Very restful things to be on Sunday mornings."

She poured Heimrich a third cup of coffee and took used dishes into the kitchen. Merton Heimrich smoked and sipped coffee and looked at the morning sun sparkling on the Hudson. And waited for the telephone to ring. He had heard it ring several times during the night. It had wakened him. And always it had rung only in a dream. In another hour or so he'd call the barracks and ask for Sergeant Kojian in the lab. And it would turn out to be Kojian's day off. Kojian would be sleeping in.

Susan came back to sit with him. She had, she said, turned the air conditioner on. They sat in restful silence. Heimrich said, "Thank you, darling. For everything. For last night."

She said, "Thank you, sir," trying to make it sound prim.

Colonel came across the field toward the terrace. He did not hurry. On the other hand, he moved steadily enough. He lay down in the shade, which was diminishing as the sun rose higher. Soon, now, they would all three have to go into the coolness of the house, in which Mite had remained, sleeping off his breakfast.

The telephone rang. At its first exploring sound, Heimrich was on his feet and a long stride toward the door. There went their restful Sunday morning, Susan thought. She heard him say, "Heimrich," a little hurriedly. But then he said, "Oh, good morning, Agnes. I don't know. I'll have to ask Susan."

He reappeared at the door. "Agnes Fielding," he said. "They want us for brunch. I don't—"

"I'll talk to her," Susan said, and went to do it. Heimrich moved his chair back, hugging the lessening shade. Colonel raised his head to observe the activity. He decided it did not concern him, and put his head down again. They'd really have to take him to the vet in Cold Harbor, Heimrich thought. Have him checked out. Not that, now, he didn't seem much as usual.

Susan came to the door. "I told them how sorry we were," she said. "And that we wanted a rain check. And I don't really want bloody marys, do you? And it's cooler inside and the *Times* has come. It doesn't seem quite as heavy as usual. I could lift it."

It was cooler inside. And the Sunday *New York*

Times does lose weight in midsummer. Heimrich was in the sports section and Susan in "Art and Leisure" and it was almost noon when the telephone rang again.

Heimrich spoke his name into it.

"Sergeant Kojian, sir. This syringe you sent us."

Heimrich said, "Morning, Mikel."

Mikel Kojian had his master's degree in biological chemistry. He was working for his doctorate. The New York State Police was a stopover. Or a stepping stone.

"Not much residue," Kojian said. "But—you been invaded by South American Indians down there, Inspector?"

"South Am—oh?"

"Yes, sir. Curare. For arrowheads. An alkaloid. Several of them, in fact. Active principle curarine. And pretty damn active it is. What we got, after a lot of messing around, was d-tubocurarine. A little of which—well, goes a long way, Inspector. Resulting in death by asphyxiation. Because the breathing muscles quit working, you see."

"No insulin in the syringe, Mikel? Because that's what was supposed to be in it."

"We didn't find any. And whoever supposed it was insulin got—well, he got a nasty shock, M.L. First he couldn't keep his eyes open. Then he couldn't hold his head up. Then he couldn't move his arms or legs. And couldn't stand. And finally couldn't breathe. Complete flaccidity of all skeletal muscles. Muscles attached to the skeleton, that is."

Heimrich had assumed that skeletal muscles would be those attached to the skeleton.

"Would curare show up in a postmortem, Sergeant?"

"Not very clearly. Body eliminates the stuff rapidly. Why the South American Indians could eat their
kill with impunity. Destroyed in the digestive tract,
anyway. The pathologist might miss it. Unless he
knew what to look for. That helps with all poisons, of
course."

Scientists do not, often, suppress their scientific
knowledge.

"O.K. Switch me to Lieutenant Forniss, will you,
Mikel?"

"Afraid he's off duty, Inspector. Had the duty last
night. Get him at home, of course."

That wouldn't be necessary. Kojian could pass
the word. A trooper in a cruise car, the nearest he
could reach, was to go to Dr. Barton's small animal
hospital, and pick up a vial Heimrich would point out
to him. And take it to the lab. O.K.?

"The lab being me today, Inspector. O.K. Meet
you at this animal hospital and bring in what you give
him. I'll get on it, sir."

Heimrich dialed the Cold Harbor hospital. After
some delay, he got James Marvin, M.D.

No, they hadn't finished yet with Dr. Barton.
Curare? Yes, he'd pass the word to Terry Snead—
Terence Snead, M.D—the pathologist who was cut-
ting Barton up. Yes, it would be a help to know what
they were looking for. Evasive stuff, curare. Might
have to send samples to New York to be sure. Not that
Terry wasn't a good man. Damn good man. But
curare was something you didn't come across too
often.

"Not something we use nowadays," he said.
"Tried it in tetanus cases awhile back. And in shock
treatment, to keep people from breaking their arms
and legs. Tried it in abdominal surgery, to relax muscles. It relaxes the hell out of them, you know."

66

By then Heimrich did know. "Nothing a doctor would be likely to have around, then, Doctor?"

"Hell, no. Very tricky stuff. Anything over, say, twenty-five m.g.'s and—poof. Unless you use artificial respiration very quickly. No, M.L., nothing we fool with in the profession. Some veterinarians—my *God!*"

"Yes," Heimrich said. "How, Doctor?"

"To immobilize animals without inducing unconsciousness. You can't just tell an animal to lie still, this won't hurt. In minute quantities, of course."

"Yes, Doctor. In one c.c., how many milligrams, would you say?"

"About forty." He added that he would be damned.

"Yes, Doctor," Heimrich said. "Looks as if we've got ourselves a murder, doesn't it?"

Susan was not happy about it. Heimrich had not assumed she would be. No, he could not tell when he might be back. Susan was not surprised. She said, "Damn. Oh, *damn.*" Heimrich agreed with her. He kissed her and backed the Buick out of the garage. Colonel came to the kitchen door and watched. He pushed at the screen, but when it resisted he did not persist. He did woof that he would like to go along. When the car door did not open for him, he went back to lie on the floor in front of the fireplace.

Heimrich drove faster toward the animal hospital than he had driven before. He should have taken the used insulin vial last night and sent it to the lab along with the syringe. He should have had the courage of his suspicions. Somebody else might have the vial by now. Carol Arnold? Latham Rorke? Even Louise Barton? Damn! He would have a rookie trooper on suspension for such carelessness. Hell. I not only look like a hippopotomas; I think like one.

There was no police car parked in front of the

animal hospital, no trooper waiting. The front door of the animal hospital was closed. There was a sign: "Ring and enter." Heimrich rang and tried to enter. The door was locked. He rang again and heard a bell sound inside. Nothing else happened. He went around to the back door.

Roger King was sitting on a director's chair in the shade of a big maple behind the hospital. There were now no cars in the garage next to the big white house.

Roger King was reading a book. It did not look like a textbook to Merton Heimrich. A mystery novel, possibly. Roger laid the book down on the grass and stood up. He said, "Sir? Sorry, Inspector. I guess I didn't hear the bell."

It was all right, Heimrich told him.

"Miss Arnold asked me to sort of stay around," Roger said. "Keep an eye on things until she gets back. You want to go inside, Inspector? I've fed all of them and changed the cats' pans. I was just—well, waiting until Miss Arnold gets back. I'm not supposed to be here on Sundays. Miss Arnold asked me to, well, stay around. But everything's all right, sir."

A very polite boy, if inclined to fuller—and defensive?—explanations.

Everything wasn't all right, of course. Heimrich said, "Sure, son," and that there was just something he wanted to check on. And was the back door open? Roger went to the door and pulled it open for Heimrich. A very polite boy, who acted a little as if he had been remiss in guard duty.

Heimrich went into the hospital. The cats were in their cages. The big black cat hissed at him, but in a rather perfunctory manner. Heimrich felt, vaguely, that there were fewer cats than there had been the evening before. Hadn't there been a Siamese in a cage, in addition to the postoperative one in the oxygen chamber? It didn't matter.

The partly empty vial marked "Lilly, Iletin (R) 40 U. Regular" was where it had been yesterday, which was a considerable relief to Inspector M. L. Heimrich. Its presence did not absolve him from carelessness, from failure to take the obvious precautions; the precautions even the least tangible of suspicions should have made inevitable. Well, no harm done. Except in his own mind.

The other vials and bottles were where they had been in the refrigerator. The same number as before? He hadn't counted them before. Any rookie trooper would have counted them before. Slipshod, Heimrich thought. Probably the result of advancing years.

Roger King had followed Heimrich as far as the door of the operating room. He stood in the doorway, watching. "A box, son?" Heimrich said. "Big enough to hold these little bottles?"

The boy looked doubtful. He said, "You want to take them somewhere, sir? I don't know whether—"

"It'll be all right, Roger. I'll give you a receipt."

The promise obviously relieved the faithful guardian. He got a box which was a little larger than it needed to be but would serve. Heimrich took the bottles and vials out of the refrigerator, starting with Dr. Barton's own supply of insulin; starting with the partly used vial. There were three other vials with the same labels, but with their snap-on red aluminum caps in place. Then: "Distemper vaccine (tissue culture)," "Canine hepatitis vaccine," "Two-way vaccine." Clear enough, except for the last. Carol Arnold could clarify when she got back from wherever she had gone. "Modified measles vaccine." He hadn't known dogs and cats got measles.

There were several bottles of each of these medicines. There was also a half pint of heavy cream. It had not been opened. Heimrich flipped it open. Heavy cream, from the looks of it and from the smell and, finally—riskily?—from the taste of it. He left the cream in the refrigerator.

"There are some other things in that drawer," Roger King said. He pointed to the drawer. Heimrich opened it. Bottles of pills and capsules. "Filariasis tablets." Filariasis? Capsules marked for hookworm, roundworm, pinworm. You can't inject a capsule or a tablet by hypodermic needle. On the other hand, you can dissolve them. *Put into the box.* Chloramphenicol. Whatever that might be. Barbiturates. Short-acting and long-acting. Simple enough. Into the box.

And where was the trooper to pick up the box? Well, it was a Sunday afternoon. Plenty of speeding cars to flag down. Plenty of drunk drivers to be got off the roads. And miles and miles of roads to cover in the southern counties of New York, where the responsibility of Troop K ran. Not that Inspector Heimrich's authority was so limited.

"You were expecting Miss Arnold back soon, son?"

"Before now, Inspector. It was around eleven when she came down from the house and got the cat. Asked me to stick around for half an hour or so." Roger looked at the watch on his wrist. "Hour and a half's more like it," he said. Heimrich looked at his own watch. An hour and three quarters was even more like it, if they counted from eleven.

"Got the cat, Roger?"

"One of Mrs. Cummins's Siamese. Off her feed a little, and Doctor was observing. Nothing serious, he told me. Sometimes they eat and sometimes they don't, he said. And sometimes there's no telling why, he told me. Of course, Mrs. Cummins has to be careful about her cats. They're her business, you know. I mean, to her they're not just cats. I guess you'd call them stock in trade."

"And I suppose that, with Dr. Barton out of the picture, Mrs. Cummins decided to take this cat back to the—the cattery?"

Roger King guessed so. Or maybe to another vet.

"Mrs. Cummins's place, cattery, far from here, son?"

"Couple of miles. Take maybe five minutes, Inspector. Maybe not that long, way Miss Arnold drives. Not that she's not a good driver, sir. She just goes pretty fast sometimes. She's—well, she's great, Inspector."

She was also an exceedingly pretty young woman. Too old for young Roger by several years. Which did not mean that Roger King would think her so. Roger was male; Carol Arnold evidently female. These facts can supersede chronology. Which did not mean, either, that Carol Arnold was not "great," sex aside.

"You've got to know Miss Arnold fairly well the last couple of months, Roger?"

Roger guessed so; guessed you could put it that way. And Dr. Barton? So far as Roger knew, Dr. Barton had been an all-right guy. He hadn't had much contact with the doctor. Hadn't really seen much of him; the doctor had usually gone up to the house by the time Roger King came on duty as—well, he guessed night watchman was what it was. Two dollars an hour just for sleeping here, Inspector. Seeing the animals were all right and that nobody broke in. "Looking for drugs, maybe."

Also, Barton had played a good game of tennis. Roger had played with him once. Couldn't give him a game.

"I guess Carol, I mean Miss Arnold, couldn't either. Although she's better than I am."

"Dr. Barton and Miss Arnold were on friendly terms, from what you gathered?"

Roger guessed so. He hadn't thought much about it. "Only, I think she and this doctor from White Plains have got a thing going, Inspector. I'm just guessing, you know. And it's no business of mine, anyway."

"Nobody's business but their own," Heimrich agreed. It wasn't, conceivably, that simple. But it was as far as this still awkward, possibly wistful and very young man went.

Did the inspector want the box carried out to his car? The solicitude of the very young for the presumably doddering old?

Heimrich did not want the box of veterinary medicines, which weighed rather less than a pound, carried to his car for him. A trooper would be along to pick it up. Roger could go back to his shaded chair and to his book. To his study of marine biology.

"Actually," Roger said, "I was reading an old Stout. It being Sunday."

"Good writer, Stout was," Heimrich said. "Lived not too far from here, you know."

Roger said, "Did he, sir?" without too great a display of interest. "If Miss Arnold comes back to the house, I'll tell her you'd like to see her, shall I?"

That would be fine. And where the hell was the trooper? Nothing to do but wait, obviously. Eventually, call the barracks and ask what the hell. Not all that hurry yet. He had a murder, but murders are seldom solved in a day. Murder by curare. He'd never come across that before. He doubted that many had.

He went into the waiting room and sat on the green sofa. He reached in his jacket pocket for cigarettes, and was thankful that the hospital was air-conditioned. For the sake of the penned animals, of course. But the comfort could be shared by an inspector of the New York State Police.

His groping fingers did not come on the package of Kents they sought. They came on the edge of something larger than a pack of cigarettes. Of course, the copy of *The American Cat Fancy* magazine he had thrust into the pocket and forgotten; the copy Charley Forniss had unintentionally walked away with—walked away with from here. Heimrich took the magazine out of his pocket and put it on the side table, where it belonged.

He got Kents out of the pocket and lighted one. He wished the trooper would show up. And that Carol Arnold would. More than two hours, now, on an errand she had expected to need only a quarter of that time. Perhaps Mrs. Grace Cummins, owner of the Linwood Cattery, had invited Carol to stay to lunch. Mrs. Cummins had looked like a woman whose invitation would be hard to refuse.

He picked up *The American Cat Fancy* idly and opened it. The issue for the preceding January. Evidently veterinarians were no more inclined to keep their reading matter up to date than, say, dentists.

He leafed through the small magazine. There were a good many advertisements of catteries in it. One offered "Spring kittens, beginning in April. CFA registered. Show Quality." This advertisement had a photograph of a white cat with long hair. A very beautiful cat, who looked a little bored.

There were a good many cats pictured in the magazine. Most of them had the words "Grand Champion" in front of their names, which, in Heimrich's judgment, tended to be fanciful. Who would want to call Lawnside's Princess Sapphire of Kensington, ACA registered, to come to have dinner? Not that it was often necessary to call Mite. He was usually there already, waiting. If he happened to be afield, "Hey, Mite!" would fetch him at a run.

Heimrich had started at the back of the magazine and worked toward the front, as was his custom. He was about to return it to the table when he saw the title of the leading article, "Seal Point Best of Year." The article was by C. Braithwaite Lumbarton, who would also be a little hard to call to dinner.

Heimrich read:

A seal-point Siamese, Linwood's Prince Ling Tau, became best cat of the past year by going best of show in Fort Lauderdale in December. The show was that of the Lauderdale Fanciers Club, a Cat Fanciers Association affiliate. Prince Ling Tau is CFA registered.

The best opposite sex at the show was Brunt's Lady Lakewood of Lamour.

During the year, the Linwood cat, Mrs. Grace Cummins, R.N., breeder, amassed 461 points in shows throughout the United States and Canada. Judges chose him over twelve other grand champions in the various shows.

It has been several years since a Siamese won this coveted honor, and—

Heimrich stopped reading. He turned the page. There was an advertisement on the page following. It took up half the page. It had a picture of a Siamese cat, who was handsome and alert and looked to Heimrich much like other Siamese he had seen. Of course, he has not seen very many. Not many roam at large in Putnam County.

A caption introduced the Siamese cat. "Linwood's Prince Ling Tau. Grand Champion of Grand Champions. Best cat of year."

Underneath this caption was, "At stud to approved females."

And, under that, "Apply to Linwood Cattery, Rt. 5, Cold Harbor, N.Y. Stud fee $200. Impregnation guaranteed."

Well, Prince Ling Tau was being well paid for a simple, and to two cats probably enjoyable, activity. Not, of course, as much as Secretariat. But Secretariat was bigger, and could run faster.

"Breeder, Mrs. Grace Cummins." A telephone number was also included.

The "fancy," to Heimrich, seemed extremely fancy. But if someone wanted a Siamese cat, presumably a grand champion in her own right, serviced for $200, it was no concern of his. Pleasant cats can be come by more easily. Big dogs can bring them home.

Heimrich tossed the copy of the little magazine for the fancy onto the end table and looked at his watch. Almost two thirty now. And so almost five times the period Carol Arnold had allowed herself for delivery of a cat to Mrs. Grace Cummins and return from the errand.

And where the hell was that trooper?

The crunch of car tires on the gravel coincided with Heimrich's irritated wondering. He went to the door and opened it. Finally. A uniformed state trooper was getting out of a cruise car. He wasn't a trooper Heimrich knew. He was getting to know a decreasing number of the men in the uniformed branch.

This trooper was tall and lean and erect. He walked like a soldier to the opened door. He said, "Inspector Heimrich?" and, when Heimrich nodded his head, stood at attention and said, "Trooper Brown, sir. Reporting as instructed."

Heimrich said, "All right, Brown. What I want—" But Trooper Brown was still talking.

"Should have been here anyway an hour ago, sir. Not a mile away when I saw this accident. Figured that came first, Inspector. Because this fool woman was still in the car, you see. Trying to turn off into a side road and didn't have sense enough to slow down for it. Banged into a tree. I'm to pick something up and take it to the lab, way I get it."

"Yes, Brown. This accident. About a mile from here, you say?"

"About that. Side road off the highway. Linwood Court, the sign says. And there's another sign. 'Something Cattery.' I didn't know cathouses put up signs, did you, sir? Way I figured it—"

The expression on Heimrich's face stopped him.

"This woman in the car. Badly hurt? And—did you get her name?"

"Out cold, sir. Not cut up that I could see. Maybe just banged her head against the windshield. But she was still out when the ambulance showed up. Had to wait for it, Inspector. And for the Purvis tow truck. Reason it took me so long, sir."

"Her name, Trooper—did you get her name?"

"From her driver's license, sir. Not from around here. Address is in Ithaca."

"Her *name*, Brown. *What's her name?*"

But Heimrich was certain what the name would be before the trooper fumbled his notebook out of a uniform pocket and read from it. It was the name Heimrich had known it would be.

He said, "Cold Harbor Hospital, Brown?"

The answer to that was inevitable. Brown said, "Sure." He even forgot the "sir" because of the urgency in Heimrich's voice. Heimrich started for his car.

"This whatever-it-is I was to pick up, Inspector?" the trooper said.

"On the green sofa in there," Heimrich said. "To the lab. Then come back to the hospital. There'll be some things I'll want to ask you."

Heimrich's car was on the hardtop of Barton Lane by the time the trooper came out with the box. It was going fast. Inspectors can be nuts like anybody else, Trooper Brian Brown thought, as he drove the cruiser down the lane, not as fast as Heimrich had driven.

6

HEIMRICH USED THE CAR TELEPHONE on his way to Cold
Harbor and the hospital there; to the emergency ward,
with Carol Arnold probably still in it and perhaps still
"out cold." And quite possibly a "fool woman" who
hadn't slowed properly for a sharp curve—a curve
onto a road which led up to the Linwood Cattery.
Anything is possible, even coincidence.

One of the Purvis boys answered at the garage.
Yeah, they had picked a car up at Linwood Court and
NY 11F. A big Pontiac, lodged off the road against a
tree. No, not too badly mashed up. Left front fender
bashed in. Yes, Pontiac, year before last. Not much
mileage on it. All right, he wouldn't mess with it until
the Inspector got there. Wouldn't have, anyway, since
he was alone at the garage. It being Sunday.

The Purvis Garage in Van Brunt offers twenty-
four-hour wrecking service, seven days a week, to the
discomfort of the Purvis boys, who are numerous and
all of whom bear Biblical names. Heimrich has given

78

up trying to tell them apart, except, of course, for Corporal Asa Purvis, New York State Police.

The ambulance was parked in front of the emergency entrance of the Cold Harbor General Hospital. Heimrich pulled the Buick up behind it, near a sign which read NO PARKING. EMERGENCY VEHICLES ONLY.

A resident was on duty in the emergency ward along with an orderly and a nurse's aide. None of the three knew Inspector M. L. Heimrich. He produced identification.

Arnold, Carol? Yes, such a patient had been brought in about an hour ago. Concussion, apparently mild. Held for observation; transferred to Room 212, second floor. Yes, Inspector Heimrich could try to see her. Up to the second-floor resident.

Heimrich did know the resident physician who had the second-floor duty—Dr. Francis Armstrong.

Armstrong said, "Yes. Hell of a pretty girl. Lucky she was wearing a seat belt. Got quite a bump as it was. Against the windshield, apparently. But going to be all right, far's we can tell. Concussion, but apparently mild. X ray negative. No reason you shouldn't see her, if you want to. Find her a little fuzzy, probably. Just an automobile accident, wasn't it?"

And, if so, why the concern of an inspector BCI? The question was not asked. It remained implicit.

A nurse took Heimrich to Room 212 and knocked on the door of it. The knock was perfunctory; the nurse opened the door without waiting for an answer. She said, "We have a visitor, dear," and Heimrich followed her into the room.

Carol Arnold was propped high in the hospital bed. She was not bandaged; a rather large bump on her head began at the hairline and extended into the blond hair. The blue eyes were open. They seemed even larger than Heimrich had remembered them. Carol said, "Hello, Inspector. Are you going to say 'You women drivers'? Something like that?" But she smiled as she spoke.

Heimrich had not planned to talk about women drivers. He does not share that prejudice. It is his belief that Susan drives at least as well as he does, possibly better. He said, "No, Miss Arnold. They're taking good care of you, I believe?"

"Fussing about me," she said. "Have to observe me, is the way they put it. But I just bumped my head and I feel all right. Almost all right, anyway. Did I wreck the Bartons' car? And what about Lady Bella, Mrs. Cummins's cat?"

"Not too much damage to the car," Heimrich told her. "I don't know about the cat. You were taking it to the cattery when you had this accident?"

"Yes. Mrs. Cummins called and asked me to. Her, not it," Carol said. "I had her in a carrying-case box on the seat beside me, Inspector. So I could answer when she yelled. They resent being in boxes, so they yell. I had the seat belt around her box, as well as I could get it, anyway. I do hope she's all right. She's a nice little cat. One of Ling's get. I hope somebody got her out."

"A trooper found you," Heimrich said. "Perhaps he sal—I mean rescued the cat. You had your own seat belt on, apparently?"

"Of course. I always wear it. I'm really a very careful driver, Inspector. In spite of what I suppose you think."

Accidents can happen to anybody, even the most careful. He told her that. He added that Roger King had said she was a very good driver.

"He's a nice child," she said. "Very interested in fish, but nice."

80

"He also said that sometimes you drive fast."

"I suppose I do, sometimes. Doesn't everybody? But if you mean today, no, I was going very slowly. So as not to jounce Lady Bella. Also—well, I'm still alive, Inspector. And you say I didn't smash the car up too badly."

"Not too badly, Miss Arnold. Want to tell me how it happened?"

Her wide eyes widened further, and there was a question in them. Heimrich could guess the question: Why was a policeman of inspector rank interested in a minor traffic accident? She did not put the question into words.

"It's a little blurry," she said. "I was slowing for the turn—it's a very sharp turn, you know—and then —well, the car wouldn't turn. Not the way it usually does, anyway. It was as if the steering wheel had—got stuck somehow. I don't know how else to put it. So it just went on, over a sort of bank. In spite of the brake. And—I guess went into something. Was it a tree, Inspector? I told you it was sort of blurry. And then I was in bed, I suppose here, and somebody was shining a light in my eyes."

"Yes, it was a tree. You tried to turn into this Linwood Court and the car wouldn't turn. As if— would you say the steering mechanism had got stuck somehow?"

"That's the way it felt. As if—well, as if everything had suddenly got too heavy. I don't know any other way to put it."

"I understand, Miss Arnold. The car has power steering, I suppose?"

"Of course. Don't all cars?"

"All recent ones, anyway. All big ones. Nothing like this had ever happened before? I gather you've driven the car frequently?"

"Since I've been there, fairly often. On errands for the doctor. Things like that. A few times to market for Mrs. Barton. She doesn't drive anymore. Hasn't for a couple of years, from what Roger tells me. Doesn't feel up to it, he said."

"She's not well, Miss Arnold?"

"I guess not, although whatever it is, she doesn't talk about it. To me, anyway. And she gets around all right. In the house, anyway."

"Not in the hospital?"

"Oh, yes, there too. She makes out the doctor's bills, things like that. And when the doctor sends me somewhere, she comes down to answer the telephone. She's not bedridden. It's just that she doesn't drive the car. Hasn't since I've been there, anyway."

"You drive it," Heimrich said. "And Dr. Barton drove it, I suppose. Anyone else that you know of?"

"The boy a few times. Roger, I mean."

"I've noticed the car stays in the garage. Is the garage locked at night, do you know?"

"Not even closed, as far as I've seen, Inspector. Look, it *was* just an accident. I braked down to maybe ten miles an hour to make the turn, and it was the way I told you."

"Yes," Heimrich said, "apparently just an accident. One of those things that happen. I'll go—"

A gentle knocking on the door interrupted him. The same nurse opened the door, as quickly as before. "We have another visitor, dear," the nurse said. "Aren't we popular, though?"

The other visitor was Latham Rorke, M.D. As he came through the door he said "Dar—" but stopped when he saw Heimrich. He changed what had, obviously, started off as "Darling" into an "Oh."

"I'm just leaving, Doctor," Heimrich said. "Just

came by to see that Miss Arnold is all right. Seems she is."

"Just a bump on the head, Lathe," Carol Arnold said. "Just a little bump on the head."

Heimrich left Room 212. He did not think that his leaving was noticed by either of the two who remained. It hadn't taken Rorke long to hear about the accident; to drive from White Plains to Cold Harbor. How had he heard? News of minor traffic accidents does not get that promptly on radio reports, even from very local stations. Obviously, Carol had called him up. Confirmation of what was already obvious.

Trooper Brown was in his car, parked behind Heimrich's. The ambulance was gone; ambulances do not long stand idle on hot Sunday afternoons. Had Brown found a cat in Miss Arnold's car when he went to her rescue?

"A cat, Inspector?"

A small Siamese cat in a carrying box, probably yammering its—no, her—head off. On the front seat, beside Carol Arnold. Or, of course, on the floor in front of the seat. Or a broken box, with no cat in it.

"Didn't see any cat, sir."

Cat already delivered, and Carol on her way back? No. She had been turning into Linwood Court, not out of it.

Had Brown noticed whether the air conditioning was turned on in the Pontiac? Or whether the engine was running? The engine had not been running. Stalled when the car hit the tree, probably. He hadn't checked on the air conditioning. Yes, as he remembered it, the ignition was on.

"Thing is, sir, I wanted to get the girl out of there. When I found out she was still alive."

"Yes, Trooper," Heimrich said. "That came first,

83

of course. Let's go look at where it happened. I'll follow you."

It was only about twenty minutes, driving at lawful speed and stopping for red lights, to the intersection of NY 11F and Linwood Court. A hundred yards or so before they reached it, there was a sign: HIDDEN DRIVEWAY. The Court merited the demotion. It was identified only by a sign that was largely hidden by a lilac bush.

The court, or driveway, went off at right angles to 11F. It had been gravel-surfaced, but most of the gravel was gone. Brown slowed and Heimrich slowed behind him. Brown pulled the police car onto the shoulder of 11F. Heimrich pulled the Buick up behind.

There were no marks of suddenly skidding tires on the highway. Those began on the narrow graveled road. They continued into a ditch.

"There's the tree she hit," Brown said, and pointed. The tree was a big maple, and it had a gash in its bark. The near side of the ditch was scarred where something had been dragged up over it—a Pontiac with crumpled fenders at the end of a cable, being wound out of its predicament by a tow truck. So.

"Mrs. Cummins's place is about a quarter mile up the road," Brown said. "Doesn't make it easy to get to, does she? Want to go up and see her place, Inspector?"

"Not right now," Heimrich said. "We'll go have a look at the car. Dr. Barton's car."

It was another fifteen minutes to the Purvis Garage, in the middle of Van Brunt, if Van Brunt can be said to have a middle. The garage was somnolent. Several cars baked in the sun in front of the garage. One of them was a Pontiac sedan. Its left front fender was bashed in against the left front tire. Brown and Heimrich parked their cars, making sure that channels to the gas pumps were left open. Not that Purvis relied much on the sale of gas these days. A big new Exxon station across the street enticed most motorists. It was on the former site of the firehouse which had burned down years ago, on the night Merton Heimrich had first met Susan Faye—and thought her not very pretty and noticeably harrassed.

A tall man in his late twenties came out of the garage. (Or was it early thirties?) Abraham Purvis. (Or was it Obadiah?)

Whichever it was said, "Afternoon, M.L. Hot enough for you? There she is. Body job. Woman driver from what I hear. That girl works for the vet, way I get it."

"Yes," Heimrich said. "Miss Carol Arnold. Just the fender banged up? Radiator O.K.? Engine all right?"

The radiator seemed to be all right. The wheels probably would need alignment. They hadn't tried the engine. "Just towed her over, Inspector. Fender's jammed up against the wheel. Pull it out tomorrow, maybe. Could be we can iron it out, but it may cost Dr. Barton a new fender, from the looks of it."

Which Adrian Barton wouldn't be paying for. The country grapevine hadn't functioned with its usual speed, apparently. Heimrich saw no need to hurry it.

"Let's turn the motor over," Heimrich said. "Just to see. Ignition key in it?"

The key was not. It was in the office. "Just to be on the safe side, case I have to go out on a job." He went in and got the Pontiac's ignition key. He said, "Want I should try her?" Heimrich did.

The starter growled. Then the engine caught.

With the pressure of Purvis's foot on the gas pedal, the engine roared. "Sounds O.K.," Purvis said, and moved to get out of the car. And the motor died. He started it again, and it roared again. He let it run for several seconds this time and then eased the pressure on the gas pedal. And the engine stalled. He tried it twice more, and twice more the motor roared and then stalled.

"Won't idle," he said, and got out of the car. "Could be the carburetor got banged out of kilter. Want I should have a look?"

Heimrich did, and Purvis raised the hood and leaned in toward the engine.

"Looks all right," he said. "Could be it got banged out of adjustment, I suppose. I can check it out, if you want."

Heimrich did want. Purvis went into the garage and came out with a screwdriver. He leaned again toward the Pontiac's engine and thrust the screwdriver in at something. Heimrich couldn't see what, but assumed the carburetor. Purvis said, "Uh-huh!" and, "Want to try her now, Inspector?"

Heimrich got into the Pontiac and turned the ignition switch. The engine was by now resigned. It started at once, loudly, as Heimrich pressed down on the gas pedal. He relaxed the pedal. The engine kept on running, but with lesser sound. Still fast and noisy for idling speed.

Purvis said "Yup" and used the screwdriver again. The engine sound diminished to a contented hum. Purvis pulled down the hood.

"Just out of adjustment," he said. "Set so it wouldn't idle. Have to race it or it'd stall. O.K. now."

Heimrich let the motor run. The fan of the air conditioning unit hummed. Air—still warm air—came out of the two vents in the dash. The air conditioning was on; it had been on when the heavy car crashed into the maple tree. Unless, of course, Purvis had turned it on.

Purvis had not. "Told you I didn't run the motor," he said. "Didn't even get into her until just now."

An air-conditioning unit is a drag on a car's engine. If the idling rate is set very low, the added drag can stall an engine.

Heimrich cut the motor and got out of the car. He said, "This model has power steering, hasn't it?" and decided not to take a chance on young Purvis's name. Obadiah probably, but not certainly. Nobody likes to be called out of his name.

"Sure," Purvis said. "What doesn't nowadays?"

Heimrich was remembering from years back an experience of his own—an experience in a then new Buick. The engine had stalled as he had taken his foot off the gas pedal and moved it to the brake as he was turning into a filling station. And suddenly, disconcertingly, the previously responsive car had turned into a sluggish monster and the steering wheel into a thing to be struggled with. When an engine dies, so does power steering.

He might as well make sure.

"If Miss Arnold took her foot off the gas and put it on the brake," he said to Purvis, "to make this sharp turn, the motor would have stalled, you think? As it did for us?"

"Damn near sure to, the way it was set. With the AC on, about a hundred percent sure."

"And the power steering would go off?"

"Sure. She'd all at once feel like a truck, M.L. You could still steer, of course. But it would fight you. And be one hell of a surprise. You figure—?"

"Miss Arnold isn't a particularly big young

87

woman," Heimrich said. "And, as you say, the sudden failure of the power steering would come as a hell of a surprise. To anyone, of course."

Purvis said, "Yeah," with a note of puzzled acceptance in his voice. "You think—?"

"Anyone with access to the car could put the carburetor out of adjustment?"

"Sure. Anybody with a screwdriver who knew what a carburetor looks like and where to find it."

"But the engine would start? And keep on running until you eased up on the gas? The way it did with you?"

"As long as you gave it enough gas. Enough to get the car moving. Yeah."

"All right," Heimrich said. "I'd like you to remember what we found out about the doctor's car, Obadiah. O.K.? And you too, Trooper."

Purvis said, "Sure, M.L. Only Obadiah's one of my brothers. My name's Silas. Sort of a hick name, I guess. But you know Dad, Inspector."

Heimrich said, "Sorry, Silas."

Trooper Brown said, "Sir."

Trooper Brown could go back on patrol. Mrs. Barton would let the garage know what to do about the car.

"*Mrs.* Barton?"

It wasn't a secret. "Dr. Barton is dead," Heimrich said. "He died very suddenly."

Purvis said, "*Jeez,* " and there was something like awe in his voice.

Heimrich got into his Buick. He sat in it thinking. Two efforts to kill Adrian Barton, DVM? One by tampering with a car of which he was the most frequent driver, on the chance that a fatal accident would result? Rather an outside chance; entirely an outside chance, as it had turned out. Then another, and successful, try with a surer method? Possibly. At the moment, almost anything was possible. Carol Arnold drove the car, and anybody might have known that. Certainly Louise Barton would have known it. And, although she no longer drove, if it was true she no longer drove, she had driven, might know about idling speeds and power steering. And she could get around. Get from house to animal hospital. So, obviously, to the garage which adjoined the house—a garage seldom closed up, never locked up.

Who profits? The old question. And profits how? By elimination of an unfaithful husband? Or a suspected mistress of that husband? Or, conceivably, both.

Heimrich turned the switch which brought the Buick to life. Anybody might have had access to the Pontiac in its garage. Anybody who knew his way around the Barton enclave. Dr. Latham Rorke was one who did.

There are several kinds of profit. Monetary profit is the simplest and the most obvious. Did Dr. Barton leave a considerable estate and, if so, to whom? To his widow, presumably. By law, a major portion at the least. No way of finding out about that late on a Sunday afternoon.

Emotional profit, as revenge for infidelity? That happened. Profit from the elimination of a sexual rival? Not unknown. From the elimination of an importunate suitor? Less likely, unless a more desirable one was within reach. And there is the also emotional motive of fear—fear of exposure.

Heimrich drove home, considering possibilities. Which, with nothing to go on, was an obvious waste of mental energy, since theories must be based on facts

—facts which hide themselves in the languor of hot Sunday afternoons.

It was cool in the house. Colonel sat up and sat tall and, gently, woofed at him. The woof of a neglected dog. Mite, curled near an air-conditioning outlet, uncurled and looked at Heimrich, and looked upside down. Heimrich said "Hi" and got no answer. On the terrace? No. Taking a nap? No. A note under the telephone, which was the accepted place. Finally, yes.

"At the shop, dear, messing with paints. Home soon. The lab called. Love."

It was unsigned. There had been no need to sign it.

He called *susan faye fabrics* first. This time he had someone to say "Hi" to. She would be right along. She hadn't been getting anywhere, anyway. No, he didn't need to. Barney was picking her up.

Barney is Van Brunt's taxicab service.

Heimrich dialed the police lab. He got Kojian.

"These bottles you sent up," Sergeant Kojian said, "and a hell of a lot of them, Inspector. And all what they're labeled as. Except—"

The exception was what was wanted; what was expected.

The vial of insulin which Barton had been using did not contain insulin. It contained about four c.c.'s of d-tubocurarine. Oh, there were traces of insulin, but rather minute traces. Yes, the rubber plug remained in the vial.

"What somebody did, Inspector," Kojian said, "was to stick a needle through the plug and draw out the insulin. Squirt it away somewhere, fill the hypodermic with curare and squirt it in the vial. Have to do it a couple, three times, maybe. Way it was done, thousand to one. To give this vet of yours the surprise of his life. Or, you could say, of his death, couldn't you?"

No, there had not been curare in any of the other bottles and vials Heimrich had sent along. And the snap-off aluminum caps on the other vials of insulin, Dr. Barton's reserve supply, were firmly in place. And it was five o'clock, and Kojian was going to shut up shop and go home. No, the lab would not really be shut up. The inspector ought to know it never was. What was shutting up for the night was Sergeant Kojian.

Five o'clock it was, and almost time for a drink. And, God knew, after time for lunch, although not yet time for dinner. And he hoped Barney would be as reliable as he usually was.

He dialed the Cold Harbor General Hospital. Dr. James Marvin was not on duty. Neither, from the board, was Dr. Terence Snead. Well, she'd look. Yes, a note to Inspector M. L. Heimrich. "Autopsy complete. Yes, probably. Report in the morning."

Barney's Chevy climbed the steep drive. Heimrich could identify it by its cough, which was chronic. Merton Heimrich went to the door to greet his wife. She had got a dab of paint in her hair. Fortunately, fabric designers do not often use oil paint. Gouache, Susan would have been using in the workroom, which she declined to call studio, of her shop. Gouache is water-soluble. Like, Heimrich gathered, curare.

It was too early for before-dinner drinks, and it was still too sunny on the terrace. They had their martinis inside, where it was reasonably cool. They had crackers and cheese with the martinis, to make up for Merton Heimrich's missed lunch. He told Susan about Carol Arnold's misadventure.

Susan said, "Mmm." She said, "She's not badly

hurt? Not, oh, all gashed up? Because she's such a pretty girl. And that young doctor's in love with her."

Carol was not all gashed up. She was not really gashed up at all. Just a bump on the head. And, yes, Latham Rorke might well be in love with her. Summoned, he had been quick to respond. As quick as his Volks would carry him from White Plains to Cold Harbor.

Which reminded Merton Heimrich of something; something he should have asked Miss Arnold when he saw her in her hospital room. He finished his drink and went to the telephone.

Arnold, Carol? One moment, please. Miss Arnold had been discharged from the hospital. Oh, about half an hour ago. Well, the second-floor nurse station might know whether anybody had been with her when she signed out. If Mr.—if Inspector Heimrich would hold on a minute?

Yes, Dr. Latham Rorke had been with Miss Arnold when she had been discharged. The nurse who had pushed her in the obligatory wheel chair out of the hospital remembered Dr. Rorke. He had walked beside the wheel chair. He had helped Miss Arnold into a car. Yes, the nurse had thought the car was a Volkswagen. A little after four. Records would have the exact time.

It wasn't all that important. Heimrich dialed again, this time the number of the late Dr. Barton's house, and, apparently, his hospital as well. He had to wait for five rings. He got a "Yes?" heavy with tired resignation. No, he could not. Mrs. Barton was resting. Yes, this was her sister, Mrs. Evans. Somebody had to be with her, and heaven knew where that girl was, when she was really needed. Out with that young man of hers, probably.

Of course, she would have seen Carol Arnold if she had come in. Or heard her, anyway. Well, if the inspector insisted, she supposed she could go up and see. But she had been about to make her sister a cup of tea. She needed it, poor thing. Oh, all right.

Heimrich waited rather a long time. Finally, "Like I said, she's not there. I knew she wouldn't be." There was triumph in the voice now.

Oh, all right, if she happened to see that girl when she came home, she'd tell her to call Inspector Heimrich. All right, at home. And perhaps her sister would be up to talking to Inspector Heimrich tomorrow. If it was really that important.

Tomorrow and tomorrow and tomorrow. Well, tomorrow would be time enough to find out when Carol Arnold had last driven the Pontiac and whether, on that occasion, the Pontiac had behaved itself.

7

GREED FOR MONEY may not be the root of all evil, but it is frequently the root of homicide. So when he wakened Monday morning, Heimrich felt no special sense of urgency. The Van Brunt branch of the Putnam County National Bank, headquarters in Cold Harbor, did not open its doors until nine thirty. The bank, until a couple of years ago, had been the First National Bank of Van Brunt, and had opened at nine. It had been absorbed.

As he and Susan breakfasted, on the terrace while the shade of the house still reached far enough out, Merton Heimrich thought that Van Brunt was gradually becoming a branch of almost everything. Once, before he came to live in it, Van Brunt had had a post office of its own. Susan had told him that. Now it was an adjunct of Cold Harbor, Rural Route 5, known as Rt. 5. But no resident of Van Brunt really regretted this diminishment. Years ago the community had been a farm center. Then, in the time of Thomas

Kirby, Susan's grandfather, it had been horse country. Kirby had bred Arabians.

There were no longer many horses in that southern area of Putnam County. The nearest hunt was across the county line in northern Westchester. Van Brunt had become—what? A widening in the road; a dormitory community for those who did not too much mind a tedious commute. Or who had to go to city offices only two or three times a week. A place for a branch bank.

Where, of course, Adrian Barton, DVM, might not have banked. He had lived almost as close to Cold Harbor as to Van Brunt. And his bank might well have been in New York City. Well, the only thing to do would be to go and ask.

It was a quarter of nine when Merton reached toward the coffeepot, having his third cup in mind. But Susan was already lifting the pot. She poured into his cup. This was the black one. The first two were, to a diminishing degree, creamed. Black to start was too vigorous an awakening for a still sleepy stomach. And the first cigarette of the day went with black coffee. Heimrich had just lighted it when the telephone rang.

Susan would get it. He was to finish his coffee. If it was the barracks, which probably it wasn't, she'd tell it Inspector Heimrich was on his way. Right?

"Tell them I'll be late," Heimrich said. "Or that I'll call in. Or ask Charley to call me. I'll—"

He did not finish, because Susan was already in the house and at the telephone.

She said, "Yes?" and then, "Yes, he is, Doctor. I'll get him."

Dr. Marvin, presumably, with a summary of the autopsy report. Heimrich took a final gulp of coffee and was in the house. "Dr. Rorke," Susan said, and held the receiver out for him. Heimrich said, "Good morning, Doctor."

"Sorry to bother you at home, Inspector. But the thing is, I'm worried. About Carol. Thing is, I can't get in touch with her. And I told her I'd call this morning to see, well, if she's all right. No reason to think she isn't, actually. But—well, she got quite a whack on the head."

"I understand," Heimrich said. "You've been trying to reach her on the phone, I take it. And had no luck?"

"The size of it," Rorke said. "Not at the Barton house. I finally got this Mrs. Evans to go up to Carol's room. Took a bit of doing. Not a particularly accommodating woman, Mrs. Evans isn't. From what I've seen of her, that is. And—well, she seems to have sort of a grudge against Carol. Maybe because Carol's so young and beautiful and, of course, Mrs. Evans isn't."

"Beautiful," Heimrich thought, was possibly a touch excessive. Or perhaps not; to Latham Rorke evidently not—to Rorke, the obvious and only word.

"Anyway," Rorke said. Anyway, Carol Arnold was not in her room. There was no evidence she had spent the night there—nor conclusive evidence she had not. Rorke had tried the animal hospital, which had a direct line, as well as an extension from the house phone. He had not expected much, since the phone would have rung in the hospital when it rang in the house.

After a number of rings, the hospital phone had been answered. "By this kid who stays there nights, Inspector. Roger something."

"King," Heimrich told him.

Anyway, Carol Arnold wasn't there. So far as

King knew, she hadn't been. Not since four thirty or five yesterday, when Dr. Rorke had brought her back. "You had about then, Doctor?"

"Yes. From the hospital. When she insisted on it. I thought she shouldn't; should stay there for observation a while longer. Concussion, well, it can be sort of tricky, Inspector. But the resident thought it would be all right, and he's had more experience than I have. Also, of course, it's his hospital and she was his patient."

"Yes," Heimrich said. "Go on, Doctor."

There wasn't much to go on with, Rorke said. He had driven her to the Barton place in his Volks. Yes, she had seemed all right. And he had the emergency-ward duty, starting at six. "With one of the residents, of course."

And when Rorke left Carol at the animal hospital, she had seemed all right? Not dazed, or anything?

She had seemed all right. "Think I'd have left her if she hadn't seemed all right?"

But he had telephoned this morning to make sure? Because he had some lingering doubt?

"Not really," Rorke said. "Just—well, I suppose I wanted to be sure. Entirely sure, you know. And to talk to her. Ask if she still had a headache. And if the cat was all right."

"*The* cat, Doctor? Or, the cats at the hospital?"

"Driving back from Cold Harbor, she said, 'You poor little cat.' She said it several times, as if she were talking to herself. You know what I mean. Or perhaps to some cat. I don't know. But, well, thinking it over, I guess I got worried. Concussion does strange things sometimes. And—can you find out if she's all right, Inspector?"

Heimrich could try, would try. And when he did

find the missing girl, he would ask her to call Rorke. At the White Plains hospital? "Where else, Inspector? I'm an intern, remember."

And, Heimrich told him, one who was, almost certainly, worrying needlessly. Heimrich hung up, hoping he was right. Probably he was; probably Carol Arnold had merely gone out on an errand. To buy aspirin, perhaps. She might well need aspirin. Only, gone out on foot? The Purvis garage was usually quick and efficient. The Pontiac would, with the crumpled fender pulled out from the tire, probably be usable, if certainly not handsome.

He would check up on Miss Arnold on his way to the bank. He strapped on his gun and put a light jacket on to cover it, and to be suitably garbed as a senior police officer going to ask questions of a bank manager. A jacket would be appropriate even if the bank was only a branch.

He was on his way to the door when the telephone rang. He answered it by saying "Heimrich."

"Morning, M.L. Nothing very hot, but I thought it might fit in. A Mrs. Robert Evans has reported her car stolen. Came on it more or less by accident, reading through the routine stuff. But, parked on the premises of Dr. Adrian Barton. Way it came through. Around seven this morning, theft got the squeal."

Charley Forniss had better go on.

There wasn't much further to go on with. The car was a red Volkswagen sedan, vintage of 1974. No, Mrs. Evans didn't remember the license number. Who remembers license numbers? No, she couldn't look the number up, because the registration certificate was in the glove compartment. Well, no, she didn't think she had taken the ignition key out when she parked the car. After all, she'd parked it right in front of her sister's house. Yes, she had discovered the car was missing about six thirty, when she had opened the door to see what kind of day it was going to be. No, she hadn't heard the car start up during the night. She had been sleeping in one of the beds in her sister's room, which was at the back of the house.

And how, Mrs. Evans had asked the sergeant who took the squeal, was she expected to get home, because, after all, she did have a husband? And the Bartons' car was at the garage. Because that girl is such a bad driver.

"Better get the cruise boys on it," Heimrich said. "Red 1974 Volks. License unknown, but you can get it from the Motor Vehicle Bureau—listed under Robert Evans. Probably driven by a blond in her early twenties. Do not apprehend. No charges. Just—well, have them ask her to drive back to the Bartons'. Yes, tail her to see she does."

"No APB, M.L.? Car theft?"

"Not yet, Charley. And I doubt it's really car theft. Car borrowing's more like it. Know anybody in Ithaca, Charley? Where Cornell is?"

Charles Forniss knows somebody almost everywhere. But for once he disappointed Heimrich. He couldn't think of anybody he knew in Ithaca, New York. There would be, of course, a State Police substation there, or nearby.

"Mmm. Well . . . tell you what, Charley. Suppose you drive up yourself and ask around." About Carol Arnold, who's a student at the vet school. About Adrian Barton, DVM, graduate of the school and licensed veterinarian.

"Anything you can get, Charley. Because it's murder one on Barton, apparently."

"Thing is, M.L., it's summer vacation. May not be anybody around."

"Reason I want you to go yourself, Charley. Not

leave it to the troops. And there's a chance Miss Arnold herself may show up, wouldn't you say? She lives in Ithaca, apparently. Driver's permit issued there. Get her address that way. O.K.?"

O.K. But there was that Abernathy matter.

That could wait for a day or so. It wasn't murder one. Murder comes before breaking and entering, even when the enterer exits with jewelry worth a good many thousands. Which should have been put in a safe-deposit box in the first place. Thinking of banks—

No. A girl and a red Volkswagen came first. He drove to the Barton animal hospital. The hospital door was locked. Beyond it, a dog barked. Then several dogs barked. Heimrich went around the brick building and up to the white frame house. There were no cars in the garage; no red Volks standing in front of it.

Apparently his approach had been watched from a window. He was still some distance from the house when the door opened. Mary Evans came out first. Her sister came after her. They stood side by side and looked at Heimrich, who said, "Good morning."

"Well," Mary Evans said, "It's about time, Inspector. But where is it?"

He assumed she was speaking of her car. They hadn't found it yet. They would, he was certain.

"And with that girl in it," Louise Barton said.

There was nothing the matter with her voice this morning. It was a little like her sister's; had the same demanding quality in it. Standing together, there was a family resemblance between the two. Mrs. Evans was the heavier, but her sister did not, today, look as frail as Heimrich had at first thought her. Also, Louise had once, he thought, been a pretty woman. He doubted the sister had.

"You think so, Mrs. Barton?" Heimrich said. "Why?"

"Because it would be like her," the slighter woman said. Then her sister said, "You wouldn't believe what Lou has had to put up with, Inspector."

"Waiting on her hand and foot," Mary Evans said. "Cooking her meals. Making her bed."

"Now, Mary," Louise said. "It wasn't quite that way. She did make her own bed. It's only, if Adrian had to have somebody, I'd rather it had been a man. Like last summer. Ralph was really quite a nice boy. And I don't see why girls want to be veterinarians, anyway."

"I," Mary Evans said, "don't see why dear Adrian had to have anybody."

"Now, Mary, you mustn't talk like that. My dear husband knew what he needed. And I'm afraid I haven't been able to help much the last few years. You know how it's been, dear. What with one thing and another."

Heimrich, feeling that this discussion might go on indefinitely from one thing to another, interrupted. He said, "About your car, Mrs. Evans? You'd left it unlocked, you think? Out here by the house? And this morning it was gone?"

"I'm afraid I did leave the key in it. I thought it would be safe here if anywhere."

"And, during the night, you didn't hear it start up?"

"We were both in my sister's bedroom. I couldn't bear to have her there alone at a time like this. And the bedroom's at the rear of the house. And after I was sure Lou was asleep, that the pill had worked, I—well, I took one myself. Not that I usually do. They're habit-forming, whatever you say."

Heimrich hadn't planned to say anything about sleeping pills. He said "Mmm" in agreement and then, "So neither of you heard anything?"

Neither of them had.

"We'll find your car, Mrs. Evans," he said. "And I can have a car come and take you home. Where is that, incidentally?"

"Cold Harbor, of course. And my husband's coming for me. In our other car. The Cadillac."

A rather marked disparity in cars, Heimrich thought, and again promised that they would do everything possible to recapture the little red Volks. And that Mrs. Evans would be notified as soon as there was any news. And, if he could have her address in Cold Harbor? And her telephone number?

He got both. He turned back toward the hospital. Roger King was sitting in the shade outside it. As before, he was reading a book. And as before, he put the book face down on the grass as Heimrich approached. He stood up. Heimrich said, "Good morning, Roger. Keeping you on, I see."

"Good morning, sir. Yes, Mrs. Barton asked me to stay around until Miss Arnold gets back. To keep an eye on the animals, you know. Until their owners come to get them."

"Speaking of Miss Arnold," Heimrich said. "When she came back here yesterday afternoon with Dr. Rorke, how did she seem to you?"

"Seem, Inspector? How do you mean?"

"Oh, dazed or anything. She had a bad bang on the head."

Young King had seen the bad swelling on her head. But otherwise, she had seemed much as usual. She had said "Hi" as she usually did. Then she and Dr. Rorke had talked a few minutes and Roger had gone back to his night watchman's room.

No, he had not heard Dr. Rorke's car start up and move off. It must have done, of course, because when he came out in about half an hour—"to go to the bathroom, sir"—the doctor had gone, and so had Miss Arnold. He had supposed she'd gone up to the house.

"Apparently she hadn't," Heimrich said. "Have you any idea where she might have gone?"

Possibly to the doctor's office. She sometimes helped out there. Acted, part of the time, as the doctor's secretary. When, he gathered, Mrs. Barton didn't feel up to it. But he didn't really know. "Like I said, sir, I just stay here nights. Feed the animals sometimes. Change the cats' litter pans. See that the dogs can get out to their runs. That sort of thing. If one of the animals seems to be getting sick, I call the doctor at the house. And he comes down. That's the way it used to be, anyway."

"Yes, I see," Heimrich said. "Dr. Barton never spent the night down here?"

Once in a long while, the doctor had. When there was a very sick animal he didn't want to leave. It almost never happened; perhaps four or five times since Roger King had worked there.

"He's got a room the other side of the hall, Inspector. I mean the other side of the hall my room's on. There's a bed in it. A cot, anyway. But, like I say, he almost never used it since I've been here."

"Miss Arnold might conceivably have used the room last night? Instead of going up to the house. To, well, sort of keep out of the way. Not bother Mrs. Barton?"

Roger didn't know. As far as he did know, Miss Arnold had never used Dr. Barton's office bedroom.

"Let's just have a look," Heimrich said, and followed the somewhat gangling youth into the hospital.

The door to Barton's emergency bedroom was on

the opposite side of the hallway from young King's door. It was closer to the animal wards. King opened the door.

It was a small room, almost completely occupied by a bed. The bed was by no means a cot. It was a double bed. And, it had been slept in. The sheet and summer blanket were thrown back; there was the imprint of a head on the rumpled pillow.

"Last Friday, son," Heimrich said. "Was that one of the nights the doctor stayed here, do you remember?"

It had not been. Last Friday night, the doctor and Miss Arnold had walked up to the house together, after office hours. He had seen them just as he arrived.

"By the way, Roger, do you come here by car? Drive yourself, I mean?"

"I haven't got a car, sir. Yet, I mean. Dad drives me over, when he's free. If he's not, I walk. It's only a couple of miles or so."

"Friday night?"

"Dad drove me. He usually gets home early on Friday nights. In the summer, anyway."

"Then he would have seen Dr. Barton and Miss Arnold walking up to the house, when you did?"

Roger King supposed so. He could ask his father, if it was important.

It was not; anyway, not yet. There was no reason to question the accuracy of the boy's memory.

Barton had not slept in the big double bed Friday night. Saturday and Sunday night he had slept in the morgue of the Cold Harbor General Hospital. Earlier in the week, and the bed not made up? Possible, of course.

It turned out not to be. Roger was quite certain that no emergency had kept Dr. Barton at the hospital during the previous week. And on Friday the cleaning woman came and went over everything. "She makes up my bed every week; it's always fresh Friday night. She does the doctor's too, if it needs it."

So, a hundred to one Carol Arnold had slept in the bed the night before. For part of the night, anyway.

"Last night, Roger, did you hear anything you wouldn't have expected to hear? After you had gone to bed, I mean? A car starting up, say? Or a toilet flushing? Anything that would indicate there was someone else here? Or leaving here?"

Roger King had not. "Of course, I guess I sleep pretty soundly, sir. Only I set the alarm for one o'clock and go and check on the animals. Then I go back to sleep. You think Miss Arnold might have stayed here last night, Inspector?"

Heimrich did. And that the Van Brunt branch of the Putnam County National Bank had been open for half an hour or so. And that Lieutenant Charles Forniss probably was well on his way to Ithaca, New York.

Heimrich went to his car.

8

HEIMRICH PARKED THE BUICK in the almost empty lot
of the Old Stone Inn, which is closed on Mondays, and
crossed Van Brunt Avenue to the Van Brunt branch
of the Putnam County National Bank. The bank had
not only been absorbed, it had been reconstituted. The
four tellers no longer occupied cages. They sat behind
a counter, separated from one another only by low
railings. Each had his or her name on a small marker
in front of his segment of the counter. The counter
ran along one side of a long and moderately narrow
room, with stand-up desks on the other. Three of the
tellers, all women, had bright Monday faces. The
fourth, male, had a dour Monday look. When Heimrich went in, none of the tellers was busy.

Heimrich does not often visit the Van Brunt
branch of the Putnam County National Bank. He
mails in his salary checks to the Heimrichs' joint account. Personal visits to the bank, as to draw out cash,
are made by Susan, whose shop is only a few doors
away.

106

Heimrich walked down the narrow room to a desk outside a railing. The desk was occupied by a gray-haired woman, identified by a sign which read "Mrs. Winifred Gleason." Heimrich did not know Mrs. Gleason, who said, "Good morning, sir. May I help you?"

Heimrich told her who he was, and that he would like to see the bank manager.

"I think Mr. Tootle is free," she said. "Just a moment, Inspector."

She used the telephone, and it rang at a desk beyond the railing—one of four desks, but the one in a commanding position. She could, Heimrich thought, merely have stood up and waved at the pink-faced, quite young man at the commanding desk. Mr. Tootle spoke one word into the telephone, and Mrs. Gleason said, "You're to go right in, Inspector. Mr. Tootle is free at the moment. He's the one standing up."

The pink-faced man was standing up behind his desk. He was not standing tall nor standing thin. He was a round, small man, and his hair was rather the color of his face. Mrs. Gleason pressed a button, and there was a click in the railing gate. Heimrich went through the gate and to the waiting bank manager— J. Luther Tootle, according to a marker on his desk. "J. Luther Tootle, Vice-President."

Tootle held out his hand, which Heimrich accepted. Tootle said, "Good morning, sir. Stays warm, doesn't it?"

Heimrich agreed it stayed warm, although he would have said "hot." "Hot" would have seemed excessive, Heimrich assumed, to a bank manager, even to one as jovial and youthful as this one seemed. Heimrich sat in an indicated chair.

"So, Inspector," Tootle said. "How can I help you? A police inspector, isn't it? Not a bank inspector." He laughed when he said that. When J. Luther Tootle laughed, he said, "Ha, ha," which was new in Heimrich's experience.

"State Police," Heimrich said. "My wife and I have an account here, Mr. Tootle."

Tootle's face grew properly grave at this information. Money was a grave matter. He said, "Is there some question about your account, sir?" He looked somewhat as if there had better not be.

"None at all," Heimrich said. "Quite another matter. Did Dr. Barton bank here? Dr. Adrian Barton."

"A very sad thing," Tootle said. "A tragic thing, one might say. Am I to take it that this is an official inquiry? Related to Dr. Barton's sudden death?"

He was to take it so.

"A fine man, Dr. Barton was," Tootle said. "And an excellent veterinarian. Took wonderful care of my wife's dog a few months back. She's a Pekinese, you know. Very delicate little animals, you know."

Heimrich said, "Mmm," and thought that a Peke was somehow appropriate. He said, "Dr. Barton had an account here, Mr. Tootle?"

"Well," Tootle said, "our depositors' relations with the bank are confidential, Inspector. I would have to consult the main office, I'm afraid."

"This is, as I said, an official inquiry," Heimrich said. "Into, quite possibly, a murder. But consult Cold Harbor if you have to, by all means."

Tootle said, "Then if you'll excuse me for a minute, Inspector," and got up from his desk and went farther toward the end of the long room and opened a door marked, "J. Luther Tootle, Vice-President." He went into his private office, where, obviously, matters of importance were considered—such as getting instructions from higher-ups.

He was gone only briefly. Presumably there was a direct line connection between Van Brunt and Cold Harbor. He sat again at his desk. He moved a marigold in the vase on his desk, bringing it in better symmetry with other marigolds. He said, "Yes, Dr. Barton had an account with us. Not, er, very sizable. Four figures only. In his personal checking account, I mean. And a joint account with Mrs. Barton. And, I'm told, several savings certificates. Of course, Mrs. Barton is one of the Colby sisters, you know."

He stopped and looked intently at Heimrich, his expression that of a man who expects reaction—like, possibly, a galvanized leap from a chair, or a collapse into it.

For a moment, Heimrich felt no reaction at all, which was faintly embarrassing. Then, belatedly, he got one. It did not make him leap from his chair, but it was interesting.

"You mean the Colby Castle Colbys," he said.

"Indeed yes," Tootle said. "Yes, indeed, sir."

The "Colby Castle," which is not a castle, is a landmark. It stands overlooking the Hudson a few miles north of Cold Harbor. There is, to be sure, a turret at one end of it which might be considered a watchtower. The turret appears to be an afterthought. It is, nevertheless, a mansion rather than a castle. It is pre-Revolutionary, the onetime dwelling place of a patroon. Who had not been named Colby.

Heimrich checked his memory for what Susan had told him of the Colbys and their acquired mansion. Colbys had still been living in it in the time of Susan's grandfather. One Amos Colby had bought it, Susan did not know from whom, shortly after the Civil War. During the war, he had been a supplier to the Union army. Of uniforms, Susan had thought. Made, she supposed, of shoddy. Whatever the quality of the uniforms, the fortune they had brought Amos Colby had evidently not been shoddy.

"His son wanted to be lord of the manor," Susan had told Merton Heimrich one evening on the terrace. "From what grandfather told me, when I was a little girl, the manor had other ideas. He, the son, wasn't, as they say, accepted. Not by the people who counted." Her inflection had put quotations around the "who counted," Heimrich remembered. "My people were awful snobs, I guess," she had added. "Along with the other old families." Again, her inflection had provided quotes.

A much more recent Colby, presumably the father of Louise Barton and Mary Evans, had sold the mansion, in the thirties, to a corporation—Landmarks Preservation, Inc.—which conducted tours of the ancient building at three dollars a person a tour, or something like that. It was generally assumed in the community that, even in depression times, the current Colby had received a moderate fortune from the sale of the mansion and the land around it. And that whatever he got had been added to an already considerable fortune. And that Colby—Jonathan?—had died some ten years ago, leaving only female offspring.

Which would explain the Cadillac. Which also at least minimized a possible motive. Still—

"Do you happen to know, Mr. Tootle, whether the bank is named executor in Dr. Barton's will?"

Tootle did not. Yes, conceivably, the head office might. If, of course, Dr. Barton had made a will. Some people didn't. At this thought, Tootle's voice became markedly dolorous. Barton's lawyer would know. If, of course, he had a lawyer. No, J. Luther Tootle had no idea who this potential attorney might be. He had no reason to think the head office would be better informed.

110

Heimrich thanked Mr. Tootle, who was very glad if he had been able to be of some help, and left the bank and found a telephone. He dialed the number listed for "Barton Adrian DVM Res" and waited while a telephone rang. After it had rung four times, he got "Dr. Barton's office" in a male voice and, more faintly, "Yes?" The "yes" was female and long-suffering. Then he heard, "I'm sorry, Mrs. Barton. I didn't know whether—"

"It's all right, boy," Mrs. Barton said. So there was a "Res" extension in the hospital—picked up by Roger King. "People will keep calling. Who is it?"

Heimrich told her who it was. He got, "Oh, *you* again."

"Yes, Mrs. Barton. Miss Arnold hasn't returned, I gather?"

"Nor my sister's car. Which you were going to find for her."

"Her husband came to pick her up?" He did not add, "in the Cadillac."

Her husband had, although it had been inconvenient. "Anyway, he said it was. Grumbled about it."

Heimrich was sorry. They expected soon to recover Mrs. Evans's Volks. And would Mrs. Barton give him the name of Dr. Barton's lawyer? Why should she? "Part of the routine, Mrs. Barton. Help us clean up details of this—tragic event." Tragic? Well, he supposed so.

"Aren't I being bothered enough, Inspector? People calling up all the time. Asking about their animals. Oh, and to say how sorry they are, of course."

Heimrich understood hers was a very trying time. And the name of the lawyer? Their lawyer, he assumed.

"Miss Goldman was his. Not mine. She's Jewish.

111

Calls herself 'Miz'—M-S, I mean. That newfangled womens' lib stuff, sounds like to me."

Well, Mrs. Barton was a recent widow. One had to make allowances—try to, anyway. And where could he get in touch with Ms. Goldman, attorney at law?

Cold Harbor, she thought. Couldn't he look it up? He could look it up. And they would keep looking for Mrs. Evans's car.

(And for a pretty girl named Carol Arnold. And, come to think of it, for a Siamese cat, missing since delivery to her owner had been interrupted by an automobile accident.)

"Goldman A atty" was listed in the directory. Heimrich drove to the Cold Harbor address given. He kept wondering about the cat missing, carrying case and all, from a mildly wrecked Pontiac—an intentionally wrecked Pontiac. (Cold Harbor was, loosely, on the way to the barracks, where Forniss would call first from Ithaca.)

The office of A. Goldman, atty., was on the second floor of a five-story building on Main Street. A dairy bar was on the ground floor. There was an elevator, but Heimrich climbed stairs instead. Yes—A. GOLDMAN on a ground-glass door panel. A pretty young woman at a reception desk. Ms. Goldman was with a client. If Mr.—"Oh, Inspector"—Heimrich cared to wait. It probably would not be a long wait. He could sit right over there. It really shouldn't be *too* long.

It was only about fifteen minutes. Heimrich speculated about a missing cat. Among other things.

"Miz Goldman will see you now, Inspector."

Ms. Goldman was in her mid-thirties, at a guess. She was blond and wore a black dress which, on her,

112

was not a severe black dress. She was a very handsome young woman. She stood up behind an uncluttered desk and said, "Inspector Heimrich? I've been rather expecting you. Or someone like you. May I see your credentials?"

She might, and did.

"About Adrian, I suppose," she said. "The poor dear man. So sudden. I gather the police think he was killed, don't they?"

"We think he may have been, Miz Goldman. He was careful about the z sound.

"I know," she said. "I think it's silly, too. On the other hand, my marital status is nobody's business but my own, is it? But 'Miss' is all right, if you'd rather. It's M. L. Heimrich, isn't it? I've heard of you. M. L. the way I'm merely A.? Parents are inconsiderate, aren't they? Imagine 'Angela.' "

She smiled and Heimrich smiled back. He said, "All right. Imagine 'Merton.' "

She made a slight face of agreement. A lively and engaging young woman, Merton Heimrich thought.

She said, "Cui bono, I suppose? Nobody very excessively, at a guess. But here it is."

She opened a top drawer of her desk and took a folded, blue-covered document out of it. She slid the document across the desk to Heimrich. She said, "You see, I did expect you, Inspector. All ready for probate."

The will of Adrian Barton, deceased, was a short and simple will. Except for three specified bequests, the bulk of his estate went to "my dear wife, Louise Barton."

Roger King was to receive a thousand dollars, "to aid him to continue his education." Ralph Connors was to get five times that much, "to help defray the costs of his education." And "To Carol Arnold, so that she may learn to treat horses, the sum of Five Thousand Dollars ($5,000) in cash."

"That codicil was added last week."

A. Goldman was named as executor of the estate.

"Did Dr. Barton give you any idea who this Ralph Connors is, Miss Goldman?"

"Yes. Adrian and I were—well, friends, Inspector. Not just lawyer and client. He did tell me things he didn't need to. Connors is a vet student at Cornell, and Adrian had him down at the hospital last summer. To help and to get practical experience. 'Fieldwork,' the university calls it. And gives credit for it, I understand. Adrian had been doing that for several years, he told me. Inviting people down he considered promising students. He's—he was—a very dedicated veterinarian, Inspector. Had a thing about animals."

"Only four-legged ones, Miss Goldman?"

"Oh, he didn't object to humans. Particularly—"

She stopped with that.

Heimrich said he saw. He said, "Miss Carol Arnold this summer. Mr. Connors last summer. You said he'd been having students here in summers for several years. But only these two inherit."

"Yes. I don't know about the others. Perhaps—well, perhaps he made more money the last couple of years."

"You said, Miss Goldman, that nobody would profit 'very excessively' because of Dr. Barton's death. You meant that?"

"I was talking out of turn, Inspector. Which is a bad thing in a lawyer. I merely—well, I gathered that Adrian didn't have a lot of money. I don't know how or why I gathered that. And it's not a statement given under oath. Just a—passing inadvertence. Oh, by comparison, I suppose I meant."

"By comparison," Heimrich repeated. "I take it you mean comparison with his wife?"

"Do you? Well, perhaps. Mrs. Barton is probably quite a rich woman, Inspector. But she and Adrian— well, I gathered from him they kept things rather separate. In regard to money, anyway. There's that 'gathered' again, isn't there? Distressing from one with legal training, isn't it? But, after all, Mrs. Barton is—was, anyway—a Colby. But I'm not her attorney, Inspector. Nat Lewis is. So, if your investigation is going to extend to her, you'll have to talk to Nat."

Heimrich stood up. He said he doubted he'd need to see Mr. Lewis and that she had been very helpful.

"Nothing you couldn't have got when I file for probate," she said. "All public then, of course. Including estimate of net worth for tax purposes."

"I know," Heimrich said, and thanked her again.

She stood up behind her desk.

"If you wonder why I was Adrian's lawyer and not hers," she said, "it was because she doesn't like my name. Not the Angela part of it. The Goldman. She's, well, she's a little that way, Inspector. Of course, nobody's ever told her Lewis is a substitute for Lipshitz. Not that Nat makes any secret of it. But Mrs. Barton —well, doesn't get around very much. Nat's father is still Aaron Lipshitz."

Heimrich went downstairs to the Buick, turning things over in his mind. None of the things turned easily, or settled into a useful pattern.

Carol Arnold stood to gain from Barton's death. Not, to be sure, to gain any very substantial amount. But "substantial" is a word subject to variations. If you are broke and trying to pay for an education at an Ivy League college, five thousand dollars may seem like a good deal of money. Miss Arnold had access to anything in Dr. Barton's hospital. She might, in the

115

course of her studies, have learned about curare and veterinarians' occasional use of it. Almost certainly, she would be able to use a hypodermic syringe.

And—she was missing. She had been, now, some time missing. She had not borrowed a car to drive to a pharmacy for aspirin.

Heimrich used his car telephone and got the duty sergeant at the barracks. The all points bulletin for a red Volkswagen was to be extended to a three-state alarm. The driver of the Volks, if female, in early twenties and carrying a driver's license made out to Carol Arnold of Ithaca, New York, was to be detained for questioning. If apprehended in New York, she was to be brought to the barracks of Troop K, New York State Police, for that questioning.

That thing could, at any rate, be put in place. Heimrich was not at all sure it belonged there. He might be surer, one way or another, after he had talked to Lieutenant Charles Forniss.

Heimrich drove north. It was almost noon, and traffic was thickening a little. He did not hurry. He was not at all sure where he was going or whether, once he had got there, he would know where he was.

So. Carol Arnold a possibility, largely because of apparent flight. A young man named Connors almost equally possible, although no evidence he was in any way in the picture.

Louise Barton also stood to profit, although she did not, apparently, need to profit. Not, that was, financially. Emotionally? To take vengeance on a straying husband? Always possible. Straying with whom? The pretty girl who was a kind of intern at his hospital? Or, conceivably, a sprightly and handsome attorney-at-law named Angela Goldman? Who had admitted, or asserted, friendship going beyond

116

that of lawyer and client; who had spoken of "Adrian," not of "Dr. Barton"?

Nothing really fitted into any place in any pattern.

He turned off the highway toward the barracks.

Mrs. Barton was sometimes at the animal hospital, although, presumably, not as frequently as she once had been. But often enough to know her way around it; probably to know that curare was kept in a wall refrigerator. And certainly she would have known that her husband was diabetic and taking insulin.

The Pontiac? A second string to her bow? A faulty string, which had been tensed, in the end, against the wrong person? (Or perhaps, from Louise Barton's point of view, not so wrong a person.)

Heimrich parked the Buick in the slot marked with his name. He did not immediately get out of the car.

Things could, of course, be turned inside out. Barton might have tampered with his own car, with accident to his wife desired. For money, which he would almost certainly get. And for freedom. Freedom to marry again, more satisfactorily. But it was said that Mrs. Barton no longer drove. Said truthfully? People do not always tell the truth to police officers.

Heimrich got out of the Buick and walked toward his office.

There was still that cat—that damned cat. The small Siamese. If, of course, that was the same cat. A cat with very dark brown ears and tail.

A cat who, jarred into activity when a car hit a tree, had got out of her carrying case and walked away, carrying the case with her. Mite has taught

117

Merton Heimrich to respect the ingenuity of cats, but that was taking it rather far.

Crimes do not occur one at a time. Heimrich's In basket was as crowded as usual. He had a sandwich sent in from the canteen and tackled the In basket.

He had cleared the basket and put his initials on a good many papers, and it was almost two thirty, when his telephone rang. Charley, almost certainly.

It was not Charles Forniss. It was the duty sergeant passing on a report. A red Volkswagen of the vintage wanted, bearing the license plates listed, had been found in White Plains. It was in a parking lot not too far from the New York Central station—all right, the Penn Central station. There was nobody in the Volks. So?

"Have it printed," Heimrich said. "Then have it brought up here."

There was really no reason it had to be impounded. When it arrived and was checked out, Mr. and Mrs. Evans could come and get it. He could bring her in the Cadillac.

White Plains and near the railway station. Handy for a train trip to New York on one of the commuter expresses. They were numerous in the mornings. Three cars came from Cold Harbor, with a stop at Van Brunt—with stops almost everywhere, come to that, including, as commuters complained, several crossroads—to be hooked onto one of the expresses at White Plains. The 8:04, Heimrich thought it was. Due at Grand Central a little before nine, as he remembered. (Getting back was even more difficult, except after five. One train, he thought, limped toward Van Brunt at midday.)

But Carol Arnold would not have caught the midday train. Miss Arnold had, as it nowadays was put, split. Or, in the argot of another day, taken it on the lam. Only—why had she not driven the Volks into the city and ditched it there? It would have saved her time and been only slightly more risky. Well, one could only guess about the motives, the actions, of one running from the law. As she, almost certainly—

No, Heimrich told himself, I'm jumping at conclusions. Latham Rorke is in White Plains, interning there. Flight to join Rorke? Had they been in it together, *it* being the murder of Dr. Adrian Barton? Not too likely, as far as he could see. But he couldn't, when it came to that, see very far. Still, worthwhile checking on Dr. Rorke, discovering his present whereabouts.

He had the duty sergeant put him through to Rorke's hospital. Dr. Rorke? Oh, Dr. Latham Rorke. One moment, please. It was considerably more than a moment.

"Dr. Rorke is on duty. Not in his room. Which means he may be almost anywhere in the hospital, sir. Probably he's making the rounds with a surgeon. Or with an internist, of course. Would you like to leave a message, sir?"

Heimrich left a message, not thinking anything would come of it. If Rorke had nothing to hide, there would be nothing he could tell. If he had something to hide, he would not be likely to telephone to disclose it. And if he and his girl—almost certainly *his* girl—were in flight, he would not get the message. So—it was getting on for three o'clock and nothing from Charley Forniss.

Heimrich lighted a cigarette. As if on signal, the telephone rang. At last, Charley.

It was not Charley. It was, surprisingly, Dr. Latham Rorke.

"So you got my message, Doctor?"

119

"Message? You mean you've found her?"

"No, I'm afraid we haven't, Doctor. I've been trying to get you—I left word. No, we haven't found Miss Arnold. We have found the car she may have—borrowed. In White Plains it was, Doctor. Near the railroad station. I—well, I thought she might have got in touch with you."

There was a considerable pause.

"No," Rorke said, and his voice dragged. "She hasn't got in touch with me. I wish to God she would. The car is here in White Plains, you say? Why?"

"I don't know," Heimrich said. "I wish I did. But we'll find her eventually."

Rorke said, "Yeah." His voice was resigned. It was also unbelieving.

They would find her. Probably to lock her up. Rorke hung up and so did Heimrich.

Ithaca is a good distance from the barracks of Troop K. But Charles Forniss was a good driver, and he wouldn't stay at fifty-five. Probably not able to find anybody at the summer campus of Cornell University.

Heimrich's cigarette had gone out. He lighted another. The telephone rang.

9

THIS TIME IT WAS LIEUTENANT Charles Forniss, in Ithaca. He was, but so far as he had been able to determine, Carol Arnold was not. He couldn't be certain of that. It might take days to find out.

"I don't think she is, Charley. Probably in New York by now." Heimrich told Forniss about the red Volks. Charley said, "Mmm."

"Well," Forniss said. "A few odds and ends. Probably nothing that will help us much. I did run into a guy I used to know. Way back in high school, believe it or not. He's an associate professor now. Teaching some summer classes. Not in the vet school. English department. Magazine article writing. But he could help me some. Give me Miss Arnold's address, for one thing."

During the school year, Carol Arnold lived in a small apartment near the Cornell campus. She shared it with two other students. "Both female." The records showed that. They also showed that Carol was an

A student. The closest relative was an aunt who lived in California. No parents listed.

Forniss had driven to the address listed for Carol Arnold. The building, an apartment house by conversion, was in a rather run-down part of town. Her shared apartment was on the ground floor; her name was one of three listed in the lobby. "If you could call it a lobby." There was no answer to the doorbell.

Forniss had found a window he could look into. It was, apparently, a bedroom window—the window of a sparsely furnished bedroom, with a narrow bed and a straight chair and a table which, at a guess, served as a desk. There was nothing he could see to indicate recent occupancy.

His inspection had been interrupted. A "stringy old dame" had come out of the house and said, "*You! What are you doing, skulking around here?*"

He had explained that he was not skulking; was merely trying to see whether there was anybody in the apartment. That had got a "Huh!" Showing his credentials didn't get much more. Didn't he know this was vacation time at the university? "Those three" had gone home. Or gone somewhere, anyway. And she had not been able to sublet. The girls? They were all right, she guessed. Didn't cause too much trouble. No wild parties she knew of, and she would know, because she lived upstairs. Come back in September, if he wanted to do some more peeping.

Forniss's professorial friend had, as one of his summer students, a boy who was in the School of Veterinary Medicine. A boy named Connors. He had been due at a class which was about to meet. Forniss had met him. "A Ralph Connors, M.L."

Heimrich had said "Oh" to that. He said, "Tell you he was working for Barton last summer, Charley?"

122

Connors had. Forniss had told him that Dr. Barton was dead and the circumstances of his death, and Connors had said, "Jeez," and that Dr. Barton had seemed like a great guy, and that it was too God-damn bad. Also, "Going to blow the dean's mind—Dean Smedley's. He and Dr. Barton were classmates here, you know." Forniss hadn't known; he was interested to hear.

When Connors had told Dr. Smedley two springs before that he had been asked to spend the summer working for, and with, Dr. Adrian Barton, Smedley had been enthusiastic. "Couldn't work with a better man," Smedley had assured young Connors, and had called Barton one of the best small animal men in the country. "Could be he's the best cat man," Connors remembered Dr. Smedley as saying.

And at least once a year, Smedley had got Dr. Barton in for a guest lecture. Connors had heard two of the Barton lectures. The one that spring had been about the use of curare—"the stuff Indians put on arrow tips, you know"—to immobilize small animals without robbing them of consciousness. "To put tubes down their throats—things like that."

Barton had said, as Connors remembered it, that curare was damn tricky stuff to use because among the muscles it relaxed were those animals breathed with.

"Yes," Heimrich said. "Including human animals. Barton say anything about using the stuff himself, does Connors remember?"

Forniss had asked that. Connors could not remember that Dr. Barton had or, for that matter, had not. He felt that Dr. Barton had spoken as if he had, but he couldn't be sure.

Barton, the summer before, had seemed like "a great guy." Meaning?

Oh, a good man to work for. Considerate. Yeah,

he did keep you busy. But he kept busy himself. "I felt I was learning a lot last summer," Connors had told Forniss. "For a while, I thought maybe, after I graduate and get my license, he might let me move in with him, as a kind of partner. Pretty junior one, but it might have been a way to start." No, he hadn't said anything about this idea to the doctor. Probably wouldn't have come to anything.

A good animal doctor. A good man to work for. As a person? "Like I said, he seemed like a really great guy." During his—call it apprenticeship, he had lived with the Bartons? Slept in the house? Had his meals there? He'd got along with Mrs. Barton all right? And Dr. and Mrs. Barton had seemed to get along all right? (Forniss had, obviously, been turning over every stone he came across.)

Ralph Connors had got along all right with Mrs. Barton, he guessed. "Didn't seem too sure about that, M.L." He had seen nothing, or remembered nothing, which would indicate that the Bartons weren't getting along all right. He hadn't thought much about it, one way or another. Part of the time, Mrs. Barton hadn't seemed to be feeling very well. Some of the time, she had had a woman come in to do the cooking. Mrs. Barton had been the better cook.

No, he hadn't noticed anything that would make him think Mrs. Barton was jealous of her husband, or anything like that. He had seen nothing to indicate that Dr. Barton was, well, playing around, if that was what the lieutenant was wondering about. After all, the doc was pretty old for that sort of thing, wasn't he? Up in his forties, he must have been. "That's pretty old to a kid like Connors, I guess."

Whenever he could get away, Barton had gone over to the club to play tennis. "Only, he was a lot too good for me, Lieutenant. Old as he was."

Yes, Connors knew Carol Arnold. In a couple of classes with her. Didn't know her at all well. Hadn't tried to, although she was quite a chick. Only, Connors had a chick; a pretty regular chick. He had no idea whether Carol had been going steady with anybody. He was pretty sure she hadn't been shacking up with anybody. That was the sort of thing that got around, and it hadn't.

Should Forniss stick around in Ithaca and see what else he could turn up?

"No, Charley. Call it a day."

Charles Forniss was ready to call it a day. After all, he had had the night shift. As senior officer present, and getting what snatches of sleep he could.

Heimrich hung up. A messenger put papers in the In basket. One of the documents was the autopsy report on Adrian Barton.

Barton had been a male Caucasian, five feet eleven inches tall and weighing a hundred and sixty-five pounds. He had been a diabetic in, apparently, a controlled condition. No other organic ailments. Immediate cause of death, suffocation. Consistent with curare poisoning. Minute traces of curare found in tissues. Physiological samples sent to White Plains for further analysis, which might take several days. "Curare rapidly eliminated from tissues." There was a handwritten addendum from the pathologist. "Might have missed curare if you hadn't suggested we look for it. Evasive sort of stuff."

So, a probability still; nothing conclusive. Act as if there were. Act how?

For one thing, modify the APB. Red Volkswagen no longer sought. Recovered. Young woman named Carol Arnold to be picked up for questioning. Age, early twenties; blond hair and blue eyes, estimated weight, one-five; height approximately five feet four. (Or three.) Last seen wearing—wearing what?

Last seen by Dr. Latham Rorke and Roger King; by King last. King might be still at the animal hospital, waiting for owners to retrieve pets now lacking medical attention. Worth trying. And likely to remember; Carol was pretty and young. King was male.

Heimrich dialed for an outside line, then dialed the number of Dr. Adrian Barton's animal hospital. He remembered the number by now. And, after two rings, he got Roger King.

Roger did remember. A blue dress, sleeveless. Short skirt, but not mini. Heimrich remembered Carol Arnold's legs, remembered them pleasantly. So, clearly, did Roger King. No, no hat. King didn't remember ever seeing Miss Arnold wear a hat. No, no wrap of any kind when Dr. Rorke had brought her back from the Cold Harbor Hospital. In weather like this? A sort of dark blue dress, what they called V-necked. And Roger King sure hoped nothing had happened to Miss Arnold, because she was an all-right person.

"Pretty deep V, come to that. They don't wear very much nowadays, Inspector. Not much modesty anymore." This was not from Roger King. Heimrich recognized the voice even before Roger said, "I'll hang up, Mrs. Barton." Heimrich said, "Good afternoon, Mrs. Barton. You're at the hospital?"

"Somebody's got to be," Louise Barton said. "And who else is there, with that girl gone off some place? And people calling up about their pets, and coming to get them. Where else would I be?"

Sudden death leaves a clutter behind it—a clutter of things unfinished, things unresolved. The clutter is left to those who have not died.

126

Heimrich said, "Mmm," acknowledging Mrs. Barton's problems. He said, "By the way, we've found your sister's car. We'll see she gets it this afternoon."

"But not that girl, I take it. Since you want to know what she was wearing. Probably you'll never find her. Like her to dump everything on me and just —well, take off. With everything here to straighten up."

"We'll probably find her, Mrs. Barton. Wearing this blue dress. Unless—last night could she have gone up to the house, to her room, and changed? Perhaps packed things up? Without you and your sister hearing her?"

"She'd have to have been awfully quiet about it, Inspector. I was awake most of the night. Remembering things, you know. About Adrian and me. About —oh, about everything. I suppose she could have, well, have sneaked in. But she didn't pack up her things. They're still hanging in her closet. Or lying on her bed."

"She hasn't slept in her bed?"

"No, it was all made up. I'll say that for her, she did make her bed."

So, it had not been a planned departure. Spur-of-the-moment, apparently. With intention to return? Anybody's guess. Her handbag?

"Was her handbag in her room, Mrs. Barton?"

"I didn't see it. But I didn't go rummaging around. Just glanced in. I'd better get back to the office, Inspector. Try to make some sense of things. A lot of people seem to be owing him money. Dear Adrian was never very good at that sort of thing. And all of the records of the animals he's treated. How old they were and what had been the matter with them. Or if they'd just been boarded, how long they'd been

127

here. I used to take care of all that for him, you know. He's left it in, well, a jumble."

It must be very difficult for her. Heimrich realized that, and said so. "We'll want to go over the doctor's records," he added.

"Whatever for?" Louise Barton said.

Heimrich wasn't at all sure, but he had a stock answer to hide behind. "Just a matter of routine, Mrs. Barton. Something required under circumstances like these. So, straighten things up as you like, but don't, please, destroy anything which might, well, shed any light."

Hide behind stock answers, clichés of no meaning.

Mr. John Doe owed X number of dollars, for the professional care, and room and board, of one Towser, four years old and beagle by breed, who had had a mild attack of virus pneumonia. Shed light indeed.

"They're just medical records," Mrs. Barton said. "And bookkeeping records, which are of no concern to anybody but me. And maybe Dr. Folsom, if he decides to take over. He's thinking about it. What do you mean, 'shed light'?"

So, a cliché had turned around and bitten him.

"The last five issues of this cat magazine," she said. "The thing he subscribes to for the waiting room. Where I'd have expected them to be, because we have a lot of cat people. Not in a locked file cabinet with a rubber band around them. You think that's going to, what you say, shed light?"

Heimrich realized he was expected to laugh at the absurdity. He almost did. Still, anything unusual; anything out of place. He did manage a small chuckle of confirmation. And said that he'd stop by in an hour or so and do the routine check. If young King could stay on and let him in and sort of show him around?

She supposed so. And if there was anything he wanted to ask her about, she'd be up at the house. "Only this is about the time I usually lie down for a rest, Inspector."

It was almost six in the evening before Heimrich stopped the Buick outside the animal hospital, Adrian Barton, DVM. He had had to wait for the Evanses, yes, in the Cadillac, to arrive and retrieve the red Volks, by then thoroughly gone over and finger-printed. He had to wait while Evans kicked the Volks's tires, resentfully. He had had to pull to the side of the narrow blacktop leading up to the hospital to clear the way for a car which, at first sight, seemed to be being driven by a large and noticeably shaggy dog. It had turned out that the dog was merely sitting beside a human driver, not much larger than he and female. Being discharged from hospital, the shaggy dog presumably was.

"Ring and walk in." Heimrich followed instructions. This time the door was unlocked. Young King was in the waiting room, smoking a cigarette. He put the cigarette out, rather hurriedly, and stood up. He said, "Mrs. Barton said you'd probably be coming. And that I was to show you anything you wanted to see."

"Yes," Heimrich said. "It shouldn't take long."

He followed Roger King out of the waiting room, through the operating room in which Adrian Barton had died, into Barton's office.

It seemed orderly enough. Mrs. Barton had typed a list of names, followed by amounts—obviously amounts owed. It was rather a long list and of no concern to Heimrich that he could think of. None of the amounts was large. He recognized a few of the names. Judge Ainsworth owed $112.50, which a little surprised Heimrich. He had not known that Ainsworth, a retired judge and a widower, owned a pet, let alone a sick one. He did know that Miss Jane Pringle owned a rather aggressive tomcat, because Mite had had a fight with him. Over a female, or just because both were tomcats, resenting the existence of other tomcats.

These copies of *The American Cat Fancy*, constrained by a rubber band and kept, to Mrs. Barton's obvious puzzlement, in a locked file drawer? The drawer wasn't locked now, and King took the clumped magazines out of the file drawer and handed them to Heimrich, who slid off the heavy rubber band.

"They're usually in the waiting room," Roger told him. "For people to read while they wait. People who are all that serious about cats. He kept the *Reader's Digest* out, too, I suppose for people who brought dogs in."

Heimrich looked quickly at King. He saw no secret meaning in the young face. It might well be that Roger favored dogs. And hence the *Reader's Digest?*

The copies of *The American Cat Fancy* were those of February through June. Heimrich skimmed the earliest two. In January, there had been a cat show, in Memphis. CFA and ACA. Lawnside's Princess Sapphire of Kensington had been best of breed and, as it turned out, best of show. A cat rather oddly named Prince Tarzan had been best opposite sex. Why Tarzan? It could hardly matter.

There had been cat shows in February, March, April and May, in various cities. The winners, all grand champions, were recorded. Heimrich couldn't have cared less. He skimmed on. Various catteries had advertisements in, most of them including photographs of cats, offering stud service, having kittens available. (With papers.) Some had kittens expected.

130

Linwood Catteries, Mrs. Grace Cummins, R.N., owner, had Prince Ling Tau at stud, still at $200 a mating, still to approved female Siamese. The Prince, beginning with the March issue, was billed as "The All-American Cat." He was so designated in the April, May and June issues. Perhaps he had, the year before, earned that distinction.

But what had earned these copies of a small, and very specialized, magazine seclusion in a locked file drawer, instead of prominence on a table in a veterinarian's waiting room? Heimrich found he couldn't imagine; that he shared Mrs. Barton's professed puzzlement.

"Any idea why he kept these locked up?" Heimrich asked Roger King.

Roger did not have. And did the inspector want to look at the files on the animals the doctor had treated since the first of the year? The records for earlier years were locked up, but he was sure Mrs. Barton would have the keys and he would be glad to go up and ask her, if the inspector wanted him to.

The inspector did not. He did not particularly want to examine the hospital records of the current year. Mrs. Brown's bitch had whelped; result, three puppies. Mrs. Jones's domestic shorthair tomcat had been "neut," which probably meant castrated. (Mite remained fully male, but he was primarily an outdoor cat, and did his spraying there.) All right, Heimrich would have a glance at the current year's record of small animals in hospital, either for treatment or as boarders.

Why, for the love of God, had he told Mrs. Barton he wanted to go through her late husband's office files? Why in hell did he?

Because, until Carol Arnold was found, he hadn't

known what to do next. It came down to that. And to a final report on tissue examination from the biological lab of a hospital in White Plains.

But here he was. He might as well plod.

There were two rather thick folders, one for dogs and one for cats. There was also a very thin one marked "Birds." A parrot named Mike, property of a Robert Bruns, had managed to break a wing. Dr. Barton had managed to set it. "Full use regained." Except, presumably, Mike remained in a cage.

Cats first. Listed alphabetically under owners' names. (Except people were always saying that nobody "owned" a cat. Which was true enough, and at the same time nonsense. What you can starve or nurture, kill or save, you own.)

Listed alphabetically. Also illegibly. The records were, obviously, for Dr. Barton's eyes only; were reminders, for him, of animals treated. Not legible, very much abbreviated—down, sometimes, to single letters. "Cum. Li C." Cummins? Linwood Catteries? Probably; worth taking a chance on. "Pr L?" Say Prince Ling Tau. "SP 2½." Seal point, two and a half years old? "L.C." That meant nothing to an outsider, which was Merton Heimrich. "Ad. rea?" Again nothing to go on. "Adverse reaction?" Pure guessing. To what? There was no answer in Dr. Barton's scribble. Finally, a capital D. Which probably meant "discharged."

Below the entry was "1/23–24." A date, probably January twenty-third and twenty-fourth.

Perhaps Carol Arnold could guide him through Barton's cryptogram. Remember to ask her, when he found her. If he found her.

One other "Cum" entry: "Cum. Fe C. Ldy B 9 mo. SP. Of. Ready dis."

A couple of days ago, Ldy (for Lady?) Bella, nine-months-old seal point, had been ready for discharge, apparently cured of Of? Perhaps, at a guess. Whatever "Of" might be. Off feed? Perhaps. (People chose odd names for Siamese cats. Siamese names? Intended to sound like it, anyway. The sound of the Orient, at any rate. Of Asia. But hadn't he heard somewhere, been told by someone, that there were no Siamese cats in Siam? He couldn't be sure. In any case, there was now no Siam, so the question was moot.)

Ready for discharge? The cat, perhaps the "poor little cat" which Carol, in response to a telephone request, had been returning to Mrs. Cummins's cattery when she had run a Pontiac into a ditch and then into a tree. That *damn* cat! That damn girl, come to that.

After seven; time to call it a day. Home for dinner, for a pleasant change. For a drink on the terrace, although the sun would be slanting low. Time for rumination. By tomorrow, they would have turned up Carol Arnold and asked her to explain herself.

The Buick was climbing the steep drive to the house above the Hudson when a question which should have been there earlier jumped into Heimrich's mind.

Could it be that "D" meant deceased, not discharged? Nonsense. Prince Ling Tau, best cat of the previous year, had been at stud from January 23–24 through June. At $200 an encounter, impregnation guaranteed. As he was advertised as being.

Susan opened the front door for him, and Colonel, looking healthy but mournful, was sitting tall beside her.

Susan said "Hi" with pleasure in her voice and some surprise also in it. Merton Heimrich's hours are extremely variable; getting home in time for dinner is not often included in them. He looked tired, Susan thought. He did not look as if he had got anywhere that pleased him. She pushed Colonel aside and he accepted pushing with a mournful groan. He went over in front of the fireplace and thumped down. He didn't thump more loudly than usual. He seemed to be moving all right.

"The kids are on their way over," Susan said, after she had released herself from Merton's arms. "I said we'd feed them."

"The kids" are Michael Faye, Susan's son, but now their son, and Joan Collins, who had driven Michael down from Hanover, New Hampshire, one icy night and been just in time to involve herself in murder. She was in her last year at Dartmouth; Michael had been graduated that spring. They planned to get married in October. "When all the trees light up," was the way Joan had put it.

"Good," Heimrich said. "So she did get down."

Susan did not answer that, since the answer was too obvious to make. She did say, "You need a drink, dear."

Air conditioning was keeping the house cool. The low sun was still a glare on the terrace. It would shine in their eyes. So they went to the terrace for their drinks. Mite?

Mite had stepped out. "He decided it had got cooler."

Mite had been wrong. On the terrace it was not cooler and the sun was indeed in their eyes. But, if squintingly, they could see the Hudson River and the green beyond it. And their martinis were very cold, very crisp in taste. They were half finished with their first drinks when a Volkswagen grumbled up the driveway. (A time for Volkswagens, Heimrich thought. He was beginning to dislike them.)

134

It was Joan's Volks. She had obviously driven it down from Hanover for the weekend. And, as obviously, Michael had got her a room at the Van Brunt Country Club, where, that summer, he was the tennis pro. A room at the club went with the job; teaching and, on occasion, court rolling also went with it. Michael had more or less decided to play tennis for a living, at least for now. Until he was in his late twenties, perhaps. If he could make the grade.

They slid out of the Volks with the agility and grace of youth and walked toward the terrace. Joan was slight and short beside her tall man. She had put her hair up. (When they had first met her and been surprised that the "friend" who was driving him down from Hanover was not another male, she had worn her hair loose. It had streamed down her back to a little below her slender waist. A few more inches and she could have sat on it.) They walked to the terrace hand in hand.

The weekend of the Volks, Merton Heimrich thought. A weekend, also, of young love.

Michael said, "Hi, Mother. Hi, Dad," to Susan and Merton Heimrich, both standing—Heimrich as a gesture of courtesy and welcome; Susan because it was her job to get drinks. Susan said, "Son. Joan, dear," and put her arms around the girl.

"I'm afraid we sort of barged in," Joan said, "the way we always seem to."

She was assured they had not, and Susan went for drinks. Joan and Michael drink bourbon, in very small quantities.

"Around the club they're saying Dr. Barton was murdered," Michael said.

"Are they, Michael? Well, they may be right. You knew him, son?"

"A little. The way I do a lot of the members. The

tennis people. Well enough to say hello to, is about all."

"He came over often, Michael? To play tennis, I mean?"

Michael Faye wouldn't say often. Now and then was more like it.

"Used to be pretty regular last summer, they say. His wife came with him then, from what I hear. They got to the semifinals in mixed doubles, somebody said. She hasn't been around this year, apparently. I saw a pretty girl with him a couple of times awhile back. But she wasn't his wife, unless he was a cradle-snatcher, and I never heard he was. Seemed a nice enough guy, from what little I saw."

"Popular with the other members?"

Susan and Merton are members of the country club, but not of the tennis group. Golfers and tennis players tend to stick with their own kind.

"Look, Dad, I just work there, remember? Far's I know, he was well enough liked. You think one of the members killed him? Because he beat them at tennis, maybe?"

"No, Michael. Not that I know of. He did win at tennis?"

"In the over-thirty-fives, he was pretty good. Won his share. Maybe a little more. Good first serve, when he got it in. Ground strokes all right. Inclined to come in on bad approach shots. A little old for rushing the net, I thought. But the way he liked to play."

Tennis players are almost, if not quite, as loquacious about their game as golf players.

"Not good enough to, well, aggravate other players?"

"People like these people don't get aggravated when they lose, Dad. When they get bad calls, maybe.

136

But my flock doesn't make bad calls. Very honest crowd. Don't see too well, some of them. But no cheating calls I've ever seen."

"If Michael's going to talk tennis, Joan," Susan Heimrich said, "come and help me make drinks. Also, it's cooler inside."

They went inside.

"Maybe I do talk tennis too much," Michael said. "Bore people who aren't too keen on it."

"You don't remember anybody who seems to have—call it animosity—toward Dr. Barton?"

"Hell, no. Pretty well liked, far's I've seen. Look, Dad, I've only been working there six weeks or so. And I'm just the tennis pro—teaching pro."

"Yes, son. I didn't mean—"

"There was one sort of odd thing," Michael said. "There's a man named Drake. Blake. Something like that. Carl something. Keen player. Was club champion last year, they tell me. He did say a sort of funny thing once about Dr. Barton."

"Carl Blake," Heimrich said. "Your mother and I do know the Blakes. See them now and then. Go there for dinner maybe once every couple of months. Have them here about as often. Brought their dog over once, but he and Colonel didn't get along. Big German shepherd. Made a pass at Mite, their dog did. Colonel wasn't having any of that. You know how he is about his cat."

Michael did know. Susan and Joan came back to the terrace. Joan was carrying a tray with two glasses on it, both partly filled with a pale amber liquid. Very pale, Heimrich thought.

"This funny thing?" said Heimrich. Subjects are things to wander from, but not, when possible, too far from.

Michael said, "What?" and then, "Oh. Nothing much. It's just that you were asking, Dad."

Heimrich did not say anything.

"It was right after I got the job at the club," Michael said. "I had a lesson coming up and the kid was late. So I was sitting by one of the courts and watching two men play. Pretty good, both of them were. For their ages, I mean. One of them was Dr. Barton, although I didn't know it then. And Mr. Blake came and sat down beside me. And—look, Mother, this is about tennis again. If you and Joan want to go back and maybe mix another drink or something?"

"We can stand it, son. For a little while, anyway."

"All right," Michael said. "Dr. Barton hit a good approach shot. Deep and wide, pretty much on the line, actually. To this other guy's forehand. And the other guy tried to lob out of trouble, because Barton had come in."

The lob had been short. Barton had taken it at about the service line; had taken it with an overhead.

"Man, he really murdered it," Michael said. "Bounced it over the backstop, actually. Good smash, but a waste of effort. He had the court wide open. He could just have nudged it back. Smashes can be tricky. Anyway, he made the point. Set point it was, as it turned out. And when they were leaving the court, they came by where Mr. Blake and I were sitting. And Mr. Blake said, " 'Killer Barton, we call him. Dr. Killer Barton.' He said it to me, but loud enough for Dr. Barton to hear. Ordinary enough thing to say, I suppose. After that smash. Only, it seemed to me Dr. Barton didn't like it. Anyway, he pretended not to hear it, and he'd have to have heard it. Because I'm pretty sure Mr. Blake meant him to. Dr. Barton didn't look at us. Just walked on, although the man he had been playing stopped and said hello, and what a nice day it was, or something. But like I said, Dad, it wasn't anything, really."

"No, son, it probably wasn't," Heimrich said.

The four of them clicked glasses and drank. Mite came home from across the fields, not hurrying about it. He went to the screen door and spoke about its being closed.

The setting sun was blinding by then, so they took Mite's advice and went into the house, where it was cool.

10

THE KIDS HAD GONE BACK to their rooms at the country club rather early. At a little after ten, so Susan and Merton Heimrich had been early to bed. But in spite of that, they slept late the next morning. Heimrich was first up, and he was quiet as he made himself coffee. Made himself coffee and wondered why he had been dreaming about a dog. Dreaming about a cat would have been easy to understand; his life for the last few days had been full of cats, "poor little cats" and "damn cats."

His dream had not been about Colonel. It had been about a dog named Adrian—at first, in the dream, named Adrian. Later in the dream the dog had not been named Adrian at all, but some routine canine name which kept slipping out of Heimrich's sleeping mind. So did the dog's breed. Part of the time it was a collie; part of the time a German shepherd. At all times a big dog, and most of the time growling.

Growling, yes, at Colonel. Because—of course.

Because Colonel, bristling, had growled first. Colonel had growled, obviously meaning it, when this strange dog, collie and shepherd intermittently, had threatened Mite. Not that Mite, in the dream any more than in actuality, had seemed disturbed. (Mite is contemptuous of dogs in general. He does not relate Colonel to other dogs. He appears to consider Colonel as a rather outsize cat.)

A dream dog named Adrian. No—got it. Named Shep. A silly, routine name for as handsome an animal as the Blakes' shepherd. But that did not clear things up, reasonably, and Heimrich had gone back to sleep; to sleep until—he looked at his watch—almost nine in the morning; almost the time he was due at the barracks.

Heimrich poured himself coffee and put the Chemex on an asbestos insulator over a burner set at simmer. He went out, still moving quietly, and got the *New York Times,* halfway up the drive. There was a short piece below the front page fold. "Police Probe Vet's Death." It was unlike the *Times* to use "Vet" for "Veterinarian." It had only in the last few years stopped putting quotation marks around "gas" when gasoline was meant.

It promised to be as hot a day as the day before had been; as the day before that had been. Back in the house, Heimrich turned the air conditioning on. He poured another cup of coffee, leaving plenty for Susan in the Chemex, and was thinking about feeding the animals—who had already been thinking about it for some time—when Susan joined him in the kitchen. Susan said "Good morning" to the three of them. She poured herself coffee and said "Humans first" to Mite, who audibly disagreed. Heimrich lighted a cigarette and waited while Susan drank coffee. When she had poured herself a second cup and accepted the lighted cigarette he offered her, he said, "We don't see much of the Blakes anymore, do we?" Which was a hell of a remark to start the day with.

Susan's expression said, "What on earth?" but her lips did not. She said, "Do we want to, particularly? I think they're in Europe. Or have been. Why, dear?"

Michael had said something about Carl Blake the night before, probably while she and Joan were in the kitchen. It had started him to wondering about them. "Actually," he said, "Something started me dreaming about them last night. About that dog of theirs, really. Shep, I think his name is."

"The one who was swearing at Colonel last fall? And being sworn back at? No, I think his name was Pepper. Anyway, they called him Pep. That might have been short for something else, I suppose. Pepsodent? Anyway, I think he's dead. Somebody at the club said something about it. Last spring, I think it was. It could have been Ginny herself, I think."

Heimrich groped a moment and came up with it. Ginny for Virginia Blake.

"Happen to remember what she said about it?"

"Really, dear. What on—oh."

"Yes," Heimrich said. "According to Michael, Blake called Barton 'Dr. Killer Barton' a couple of months ago. Apropos Barton's overhead smash. Ostensibly, anyway."

Susan said, "Quit it, Mite."

Mite was using his forepaws on a bare leg, with claws sheathed, of course. Still, even affectionate cats can get absentminded. Susan said, "All right, all *right*," and fed both their animals.

"No," Susan said and sat down again. "I'm afraid I don't. I was only half listening. Actually, I think,

Ginny was talking to someone else. Grace Weaver, it could have been. The one who breeds Labs. Big black ones."

Heimrich knew Grace Weaver slightly, and that she bred retrievers. And so, as one dog person to another, would be interested in an account of Pep's demise.

"They were having drinks together on the terrace," Susan said. "I remember now. I sat down at the table next to theirs. You'd called and said you couldn't make it. You were working on something. The Roberts case, I think. And that you thought you might make it home for dinner. So I decided to have a drink."

"Mid-June, then," Merton said. "Rather latish mid-June."

"Anyway, Grace said, 'He's always been good with mine'—I don't remember the exact words, but something like that. And Ginny said, 'He certainly wasn't good with poor Pep. Must have bungled the operation, Carl thinks. Carl's still steamed up about it. Not as much, I guess, as when Pep died, but still a lot. At first, he talked about a malpractice suit, as if Barton was a regular doctor. An M.D. He even talked to our lawyer about it. And Glen talked him out of it.' That's all I remember, dear. I wasn't trying to listen. You know how it happens—a word or two catches you and then—well, you pick up snatches, without really meaning to."

Merton Heimrich knew how it happened. He said, "Glen? Glen Rivers, you think?"

"I don't know, dear. He's the only lawyer around here named Glen, far's I know. Aren't you about ready for breakfast? Scrambled eggs be all right? And bacon? Or would you rather have them poached? I think I'll poach mine."

Poached would be all right.

Heimrich looked at his watch. Nine forty. Glen Rivers might be at his office on Van Brunt Avenue. It would do no harm to try. There was at least an even chance it would do no good, either. Lawyers are sticky when it comes to discussing clients. Still—

He looked up and dialed the number of "Rivers Glen atty."

Yes, Mr. Rivers had just come in. "Inspector Heimrich is calling, Mr. Rivers."

"Morning, M.L. I enter a plea of not guilty. To whatever it is." Rivers was in a carefree mood. The mood put youth into a normally middle-aged voice.

Heimrich was not in a carefree mood, particularly. However—"Witholding evidence, Glen? Failing to cooperate with the police who are in pursuit of their duties?"

"All right, M.L. Come off it, huh? Cooperation is my middle name. Only, about what?"

"That could be the catch, Glen. Because it's about a client. Carl Blake."

Rivers said, "Oh," with a lessening of joviality. Then he said, "What about Blake?"

"Last June," Heimrich said, "did he happen to consult you about a possible malpractice suit? Against a vet? Adrian Barton, to be exact?"

"Look," Rivers said, and now there was something near to asperity in his voice, "you're not trying to tie Blake into *that*. Not Carl *Blake!* Hell, man. You know Carl."

"I'm not trying to tie him into anything, Glen. Just trying to find out what I can about Dr. Barton. Perfectly harmless question as far as your client is concerned. And I do know the bit about privileged communication. If you want to use it."

"And am I still beating my wife, M.L.?"

"Nothing like that, Counselor."

"All right. God knows Carl talked enough about it. To everybody who'd listen, probably. It was about that dog of his. Dog named Pep, for some reason. Probably because he had it. Big German shepherd. Part shepherd, anyway."

"I've met Pep, Glen. Carl did want a malpractice suit?"

"Yes. I talked him out of it. Laughed him out of it, what it came to. Even if Pep had been a particularly valuable dog, that kind of suit would have been pretty silly. I mean a purebred that'd win big at dog shows. He wasn't. Just a nice big dog. The Blakes picked him up at an animal shelter, Blake told me. So? So what? Sure, they were fond of the dog. But you've got to sue *for* something, M.L. Anyway, sue a *vet.*"

"Yes," Heimrich said. "I get your point. And I take it Carl did. What did he want to charge Barton with? Specifically? What kind of malpractice?"

"Bungling an operation. Or performing one that wasn't necessary. It was a little hard to tell precisely what Carl had in mind. Seems Barton said the dog had cancer, and that an operation would prolong his life. By a couple of years, maybe. Carl admitted Barton hadn't promised more than that. Hadn't really promised that, I gathered. Anyway, the dog died a couple of weeks after they got him home. And Carl was sore as hell about it. But you know Carl."

Heimrich did. Carl Blake, member of a stockbrokerage firm, was rather often irascible. With cause, perhaps. Stocks had not been behaving well that summer. People were staying out of the market, to the distress of brokers.

"Your eggs are getting cold," Susan called from

the kitchen. Heimrich thanked Glen Rivers and hung up.

The eggs weren't really cold. And the bacon was crisp. And Susan had made them fresh coffee.

They had finished breakfast, except for the final cup of coffee and the cigarettes that went with it, when the telephone rang. "Probably Charley," Heimrich said, and crossed the room to the telephone. It was Charley Forniss, calling from the barracks.

The report from the biological lab in White Plains had come through. "Affirmative." (Forniss, Marine Corps captain, inactive duty, is inclined to revert to military shorthand.) Yep, traces of curare in the tissues. Samples—"samples" of Adrian Barton, DVM —had been sent to the federal poison center in Atlanta for further analyses and confirmation. But Barton had died of curare poisoning. Presumably self-administered, but murder all the same.

Miss Arnold had not been found. Several young women, blond and wearing blue summer dresses, had been found and interviewed. None of them had been Carol Arnold. A good many other possibles had been sighted, one in Cleveland, one in Los Angeles. That they had to expect, and had, of course, to look into. And was Heimrich coming in? There had been a couple of telephone calls for him, one from a man who sounded urgent, but had hung up before he gave his name.

"Not right away, Charley. A few things to look into around here. Damn nebulous things, I'm afraid. Maybe around noon. Anything else coming up there?"

The last was a silly question. Other things were of course coming up. New crimes do not wait for solution of older ones.

"Nothing too hot, M.L. Nothing we can't handle."

Heimrich did not leave the telephone. He dialed information. He got the number to dial for information in the Philadelphia area. After no delay to speak of, he got the telephone number of *The American Cat Fancy*. He hung up; he dialed the number given. He waited longer this time. Apparently the *Fancy* slept late. Finally he got, "*American Cat Fancy*, good morning." Could he speak to someone in the advertising department?

"I'll switch you. But I don't know if there's anybody there yet. They come in late, mostly."

After several rings, there was somebody in the advertising department, William Cohen, assistant advertising manager. Who was that calling, again? Inspector What? Inspector M. L. Heimrich, New York State Police. O.K. And what could they do for Inspector Heimrich?

Yes, Linwood Cattery was one of their advertisers. A Mrs. Grace Cummins? Yes, that was right. And what about Mrs. Cummins's Linwood Cattery? Well, most of their advertisers contracted for insertions in specific issues, one at a time. A few, the bigger ones, contracted for a series of insertions, usually for a year at a time.

"The big ones, Inspector. Those who don't mind paying in advance for a year at a time. A lot of them —say, how do I know you're really a police inspector?"

"You don't, of course, Mr. Cohen. I could be a competitor, looking for trade secrets. But is this sort of thing secret, Mr. Cohen?"

"I guess not. As a matter of fact, we haven't got many competitors. Anyway, most of our advertisers don't want to pay a lump sum for a year's insertion. Although we do give a discount, of course. Come down to it, Inspector, not too many of them have the ready cash. Running catteries isn't all that profitable."

All right, he'd check and see whether the Linwood Cattery was one of the solvent few. Assuming he was really talking to a police inspector, who had some reason for asking. Oh, all right. He supposed he could chance it. If Inspector Heimrich, assuming he was that, would hang on a minute?

Heimrich hung on.

Yes, as he had supposed, Linwood Cattery was on a month-to-month basis. Yes, that meant Mrs. Cummins would order an ad each month for the subsequent months' insertion. Sure, advertisers could change the copy if they wanted to. If they were expecting to have kittens for sale in the spring, they would so state in, say, the February issue. Which went in the mail usually about the twenty-fifth of the preceding month.

All right, it hadn't really been any trouble. And he hoped Heimrich really *was* a police inspector, because otherwise he'd have stuck his neck out.

"Not too far, Mr. Cohen," Heimrich said, and cradled the phone. As if it had been waiting for that, the telephone rang again. There was tenseness in Dr. Latham Rorke's voice. Without waiting for the inevitable question, Heimrich said, "No, we haven't, Doctor. Not yet."

"Listen," Rorke said, to a man who was obviously already listening. "I think she's trying to get in touch with me. And that something, or somebody, is stopping her. About half an hour ago—"

About half an hour ago, Rorke had been making rounds with a resident, and he had been paged on the PA system. "Dr. Rorke. Dr. Latham Rorke. Please call operator." The paging call was unusual; interns are too lowly for such summonses.

Rorke had called the operator. "A call for you, Doctor," the operator had said. "She says it's urgent. Here's Dr. Rorke, miss. Go ahead."

There was a click of transfer, and Rorke had said, "Hello, this is Latham Rorke."

But he had said it to a dead telephone, said it to nothing, to nobody.

"May have got tired of waiting," Heimrich said. "And just hung up. People do, you know. And it could have been anybody. But you realize that, of course."

But Rorke did not realize that, and Heimrich knew he didn't. At the moment there was only one call Rorke wanted, was desperate for. So any call had to be that call.

"I know the operator," Rorke said. "Recognized her voice. I went around to see her."

It had been a woman's voice on the phone. A young woman's. One could tell. The operator had rung Rorke's room, not expecting an answer and not getting one. She had said, "Sorry, miss. Dr. Rorke doesn't seem to be in his room. Probably making the rounds."

"Can't you page him or something? Please can't you? I've—I've got to get in touch with him. It's terribly important. *Please.*"

There was a rule against it. Hospital speaker systems are to be kept clear for emergencies.

"But there was something in the way she said it," the operator had told Rorke. "So—well, so I broke the rule."

"She's a nice kid," Rorke said. "Named Ann Something."

Ann Something was sure—well, almost sure—the caller had still been on the phone when she had used the speaker system. Just before Ann had used the microphone, she had said, "All right, I'll page him. Just hold on," and the girl who was calling—"nice voice. Very young voice it sounded like. And very upset about something"—had said, "Thank you. Oh, *thank* you."

"Nobody that anxious would have got tired of waiting and hung up," Rorke told Heimrich. "It had to be Carol."

"Probably," Heimrich said. "Operator have any way of telling whether it was a local call?"

"Listen, you can't tell, anymore. You know that."

Heimrich did know that. Direct dialing has made a difference, one not to the advantage of the police.

"If it was Miss Arnold," Heimrich said, "it was probably a local call, a White Plains call. We found the Evans car in White Plains."

"Yesterday," Rorke said. "If she had been here yesterday, she'd have called me yesterday."

He was very positive, very sure. There was no point in telling Rorke that if Carol Arnold was running, as probably she was, she would have been unlikely to call anybody, even a man who loved her and whom, chances were, she loved. Running as, all right, *maybe* she was.

"I can't just stay here and wait," Rorke said. "Twiddle my thumbs. You ought to be able to understand that, Inspector. I've got to do something."

Heimrich could understand. It was easy to understand. But—

"The best thing you can do," he said, "is to stay where she can reach you when she wants to."

He was told that that was easy to say. And that it was impossible to do.

"I've got a hunch," Rorke said. "Call it a hunch. Call it a feeling. She's still up there somewhere. And *something's happened to her*. She called me to tell me where she is and what's happened. So, I'm coming up there. Because maybe I can help."

Heimrich couldn't think how. Rorke, perhaps, could help himself by activity, if only the activity of driving from White Plains to Van Brunt. Better, probably, than twiddling the thumbs, letting anxiety twiddle the mind.

"It's up to you, Doctor," Heimrich said.

"You'll be at your office, Inspector? At the barracks, wherever that is?"

"Probably not until this afternoon sometime, Doctor. Until then—" He paused to consider. He wasn't, come to think of it, sure where he would be. "If you want to get in touch with me," he said, "call here. At the house. My wife will be able to tell you where I am. Although perhaps it will only be where I was. As specific as I can be, at the moment. But I still think—"

He was not given time to say what he still thought, which was that Rorke had better stay at his hospital and be on hand for another telephone call.

Rorke said, "Right, Inspector," and hung up.

"Rorke," Heimrich told Susan. "And damn near out of his mind with worry."

"Yes. As you'd be yourself, dear. If she were your girl." He looked at her. "Oh, all right," Susan said. "If I suddenly vanished into thin air. Trailing suspicion of murder behind me. You do suspect her, don't you?"

"I have to suspect somebody," Heimrich said. "Part of my job. And Blake's no good. Even if he's not in Europe, he'll have calmed down by now, I'm pretty sure. Anyway, he'd have used a hatchet. Or maybe a baseball bat. Not a needle."

"Probably," Susan said. "Although I can't see Blake using either. Carl would just—sputter."

Heimrich thought that a fairly accurate guess.

151

And he told Susan he would be at the animal hospital. "Just poking around." Or perhaps at Mrs. Cummins's cattery, doing the same thing. And that she could tell Latham Rorke that when he called back, as almost certainly he would.

"I'll hold his hand for you, dear," Susan promised.

11

ROGER KING WAS SITTING in the waiting room of the small animal hospital. He was reading *Playboy*. He put it down quickly when Heimrich came into the room. Apparently he was not always studying, and was ashamed not to be.

When Heimrich had gone into the hospital previously, dogs had barked, resenting intrusion. Now no dog barked.

King said, "Good morning, sir," and Heimrich agreed with him verbally, although not thinking it was, particularly. Too hot, already, and too confused, too vague. He said, "All the animals gone, son?"

"All but one, sir. One of Mrs. Weaver's Labs is still here. She's sending for him. And I—I'm just waiting, Inspector. Labrador retriever, Inspector. Big black one."

Heimrich knew that Labs are Labrador retrievers, and that they run to black. For no particular reason, he went into the canine ward and looked at the

153

retriever, who was lying belly down with his muzzle on his forepaws. He turned his head and looked at Heimrich. Nobody he knew. His expression was almost as disconsolate as Colonel's usually was. No other dogs left to bark with. "Somebody'll be along for you, old fellow," Heimrich said. The big black dog turned his head away. People are all the time lying to dogs.

"Just want to check something in Dr. Barton's records," Heimrich told the lanky boy, who was waiting to return to *Playboy* until authority had gone away. Young King said, "Sir." A rather obtrusive respect for rank, Heimrich thought. Or perhaps, of course, for age. Heimrich doddered into the office of the late Dr. Adrian Barton.

Yes. "Blake, Carl. Part shep. 'Pep.' Gas. ma. Op. spec. to Ith. Prog 6 mo. Fee 75. Reported dec. 6/18."

So. Deciphering grew easier with repetition. Carl Blake's part German shepherd named Pep had been operated on for a gastric malignancy; a specimen had been sent to Cornell for analysis. The prognosis had been for six months of life, but that had turned out to be optimistic, since Pep was now reported dead. Reported, Heimrich assumed, by Carl Blake, in an indignant rage. On, apparently, June 18.

Heimrich read again the item concerned with Prince Ling Tau, all-American cat of the previous year. No man lives forever. Neither does any smaller animal or, for that matter, any larger one.

Heimrich put the copy of June's *American Cat Fancy* in his pocket and asked a last question. No, Roger had not heard anything from Miss Arnold. If he did, he would call and report. Lieutenant what, at the barracks? Oh, Lieutenant Forniss. He sure would, although he didn't expect to be here long. Only until somebody showed up for the Labrador.

Yes, if Mrs. Heimrich called while he was still there, he would tell her that the inspector had gone over to Mrs. Cummins's cattery, but didn't expect to be there long. He'd be glad to, if he was still around. Yes, he had Mrs. Cummins's telephone number. Anyway, it was around here somewhere. He'd be glad to give it to Mrs. Heimrich. If he was still around when she called.

"You know where her place is, sir?"

Heimrich knew the location of the Linwood Cattery. About a quarter of a mile up Linwood Court from its intersection with the highway. And Roger could get back to his reading. Oh, one other thing. Did Roger happen to know what Mrs. Barton planned to do with the hospital?

Roger King did not. Maybe another veterinarian would take it over. A Dr. Folsom had come the evening before and looked around. But maybe Dr. Folsom had been there merely to check on the animals still there. To decide whether they were ready to be discharged. Come to think of it, Dr. Folsom had taken one of the patients, a cat under treatment for enteritis, away with him, probably to his own hospital. Although vets were pretty leery of having cats with enteritis in their hospitals.

"Spreads like crazy, way I get it, Inspector."

The boy wanted companionship almost as badly as the big black dog waiting in the canine ward, Heimrich thought. Well, the boy would have to make do with *Playboy*. He was the right age for it.

It was not far to Linwood Court. Heimrich slowed the Buick and took, carefully, the turn which Carol Arnold had not been able to take at all in the Pontiac. There were still scars where the Pontiac had been dragged up. There was still a scar on the tree it had run into.

Linwood Court was a narrow road of worn black-top. There was nothing to indicate that it led any-where. About a quarter of a mile up it, set among heavy trees, was "Linwood Cattery." A small sign said so. The cattery was a fairly large white frame house which was a little in need of paint. Jutting out from one side of the house was an oblong structure of, at a guess, cement block. But it might be cinder block. There was room in front of the house to park the Buick. A blue Volkswagen was already parked there. Another Volks. Anyway, it presumably meant that Mrs. Cummins was home, if the Volks was the same one Mrs. Cummins had driven to the hospital to re-claim her spayed cat.

Heimrich crossed a front porch to the door. There was a window beside the door, and he thought that he had been watched through it. But now he saw no one at the window. He rang the bell. When nothing happened, except the sound of chimes inside—"Avon Calling"—he pressed the button again. And waited again. Finally, he heard footfalls on board flooring behind the door. Then the door opened.

Grace Cummins was wearing a brown pants suit which hugged her unforgivingly. She wore a white smock over it. She was a noticeably sturdy woman. "Whatever it is, I don't want—" she said, and stopped with that. She looked hard at Merton Heimrich. She said, "Haven't I seen you before somewhere?"

"At Dr. Barton's hospital," Heimrich said. "When you came to pick up the cat he'd just operated on."

"Wherever it was, I'm glad to see you now," she said. "I—I was getting terribly worried, with the phone off and all. No way to get hold of anybody, and of course I couldn't leave her. Not the way she is, could I? That hospital! I don't understand them at all. At any of the ones I've been in in the city, they'd never have let her go. Not ever."

Heimrich could merely shake his head, let his face show bewilderment.

"You didn't come for her? But you're a policeman, aren't you? She did say something about the police being after her. But she was so fuzzy, I couldn't be sure what she was talking about. Whatever hit her —well, it made her fuzzy. Concussion, almost certainly. And I'm a nurse, you know. A registered nurse. Or maybe you didn't know."

"Yes, Mrs. Cummins," Heimrich said, "I did know. Are you talking about Miss Arnold? You mean she's here?"

"Of course I'm talking about her—who else would I be talking about?"

Her hard voice carried contempt for stupidity.

"Miss Arnold is here," Heimrich said. "No, Mrs. Cummins, we didn't know she was here."

"Here for the last—oh, it must be more than two hours. And out cold except just at first. It's too bad, whatever she's done."

"I'm not sure she's done anything, Mrs. Cummins."

"Then you're not really looking for her? She said you were."

"Yes, we've been looking for her. And now, I'd like to see her."

He moved forward toward the doorway in which she stood so resolutely. She moved aside and he went after her into a wide hall. The bare boards of the flooring crackled under their feet.

"In here," Mrs. Cummins said, and opened a door on their right. "I was about to try to get her to bed,

157

but the only room with a bed in it is upstairs. I didn't know *what* to do with her."

The room he followed her into was large and furnished as a living room—a not very comfortable living room. It was hot in the room, although a window was open; hot and stuffy. No air seemed to be coming through the open window. There were several hard-looking chairs in the room and a narrow sofa. Carol Arnold was lying on the sofa. She was wearing the dark blue, sleeveless dress Heimrich had been told of.

She was lying on her back and was pale and appeared to be asleep. The bruise on her forehead stood out cruelly against the pallor of her face. Her blond hair clung damply to her head.

"See?" Mrs. Cummins, R.N., said. "She's out cold, like I said. She ought to be in the hospital."

"She was," Heimrich said. "But she apparently told you that, didn't she? Because you said she shouldn't have been discharged. That a New York hospital wouldn't have let her go."

"Something about it. About the hospital and the police being after her. Aren't you going to do something about her?"

"Call an ambulance," Heimrich said. There was a telephone on a table near the sofa the unconscious girl lay on. Heimrich moved and picked it up.

"There's no use of that," the woman said. "Think I wouldn't have called somebody if it was working? And I couldn't leave her here alone to go get somebody, could I?"

The telephone was indeed dead. It was dead, Heimrich saw, because it had been pulled out of the wall. He pointed this out to Mrs. Cummins.

She said, "So that's what she did. She must have

come to while I was out of the room. Getting ammonia, because it might revive her. Because she's not just asleep, just naturally asleep. Concussion—well, it can do strange things to them, Inspector."

So she did know who he was. Not just that he was a policeman.

"Yes," Heimrich said. "Stay here with her, will you? See that she doesn't—well, do anything to harm herself."

"Of course. I've been with her ever since she passed out. Except for those few minutes."

Heimrich went outside to the Buick. He called the hospital from there. He also called the barracks, and Susan, to tell her where he was, and that she could tell Dr. Rorke when he called that Carol had been found—found alive and that—

"He's already called," Susan said. "Apparently from a filling station on his way up. I told him where you would probably be, dear. Is the pretty girl really all right?"

Heimrich hoped so. At the moment she seemed to be asleep, deeply asleep. An ambulance was on the way.

He went back into the big white house, the almost-white house. Mrs. Cummins was not in the entrance hall. He went into the living room. Mrs. Cummins was leaning down over the unconscious girl on the hard sofa. Mrs. Cummins had one hand in a pocket of her white smock. When Heimrich came into the room, she took the hand out of the pocket and went to sit on one of the inhospitable chairs. Heimrich sat on another. It was as resistant as it had looked to be.

"A couple of hours ago she came here, you say?" he said. "In a car, I suppose?"

"I didn't see any car, or hear any car, Inspector.

Just the doorbell, the chimes. I was taking care of my cats. Changing their pans and feeding them; giving them water. Saying—well, saying good morning. I suppose that sounds silly to you?"

"No," Heimrich said, "we say good morning to our animals. One of whom is a dog. About Miss Arnold?"

"It took me a few minutes to get to the door. I didn't hurry, because I thought it probably was somebody selling something. Or wanting me to take religious tracts. There are a good many of that kind around, you know."

"Yes. About what time was this, Mrs. Cummins?"

"Around eight, or a little after. But it was just the girl, standing there. And looking like she might fall down."

"Yes. Go on, Mrs. Cummins."

"She said would I please let her in. Something like that. And 'They're after me,' and that she didn't have any place to go."

"Did she say the police were after her? Or just 'they,'?"

"I don't think I remember. I was too surprised. Taken aback. And she spoke so low I could hardly hear her. Low and muzzy. So I said, 'Come in, Miss Arnold,' and she did. There was this awful bruise on her head, you know. The way it is now."

"Yes," Heimrich said, "she was in an accident. But that was a couple of days ago. On Sunday, actually. You didn't know about that? It happened quite near here."

"No. Sunday, you say. What time Sunday?"

"Around noon. A little before noon. She was on her way here. Bringing the cat you'd asked her to bring."

160

"I'd asked her to bring a cat? What cat? Because I never asked her anything of the kind. Around noon Sunday? Why on earth would I? I'd have been in church. The First Baptist, over in Cold Harbor. Like every Sunday."

Heimrich said he saw. And what time had she got back from church?

It must have been after one. She had stopped for a bite to eat on her way back. And dear Dr. James had preached longer than he usually did. Yes, it must have been after one. Again, Heimrich told her that he saw.

"She's been missing since then, Inspector? Since Sunday noon?"

"No. She was in the hospital for a while. As you seem to have guessed. Unless she told you about it when she showed up this morning."

"I don't think she did. But she was blurry. Perhaps she did."

"Did she say anything about a cat? A 'poor little cat'?"

"Of course not. Not if she meant any of mine, that is."

"She was bringing a cat over from the hospital when her car went off the road Sunday. The cat seems to have disappeared. She was worried about it. After she was discharged from the hospital."

She did not know what he was talking about.

"There wasn't any cat at the hospital. Since—oh, Saturday night. The night Dr. Barton died. I'd brought them both home that evening. Wait a minute. You were there then, weren't you? You must have seen me get them."

"The cat the doctor had just operated on," Heimrich said. "The one you had sold."

"That one, yes. They're going to call her Jenny,

161

the poor thing. And Lady Bella. She'd been off her feed for several days, and Dr. Barton had been taking care of her. But, with the doctor dead, I decided to bring her home. So I put them both in the carrying case and brought them out. But you saw me. You were standing right there."

"Yes, Mrs. Cummins, I saw you bring the carrying case out. I hadn't realized there were two cats in it."

"The case is plenty large enough for two of them, Inspector. And, when there are two of them in one they don't get so nervous about it. They don't like to be in boxes, especially boxes that move, you know."

Heimrich could see their point. Once more, he said he saw. And he said that possibly he had misunderstood Miss Arnold when he thought she said Mrs. Cummins had telephoned her at the animal hospital and asked her to bring Lady—what was the rest of the name?"

"Bella—Lady Bella's her call name. Her registered name is Lady Mau Tang. We give them Oriental names because they're supposed to be Oriental cats. Except I've heard there aren't any Siamese cats in Siam, and probably never were. Not as we know them, anyway. They've been bred to look the way they do. In England first, and then over here."

"Well," Heimrich said, "there isn't any Siam any more, is there? To get back to Miss Arnold"—he looked at the unconscious (sleeping?) girl on the hard sofa. The girl whom conversation in a smallish room didn't waken. But he could see the rise and fall of her breathing. "She asked to come in. You thought she was wobbly, unsteady on her feet. She came in, obviously. Then?"

"I brought her in here, and she sat down on the sofa. And I thought coffee might help her, so I made her some. I had to urge her to drink it—help her, actually. Hold the cup for her. I thought she seemed, well, a little more pulled together, so I went back and made another cup. Instant, you know. But very good instant. The kind I drink myself. But when I brought it back—"

When she had brought back the second cup of instant, but very good instant, coffee, Carol Arnold wasn't sitting on the sofa any more. She had slid off it, and was sitting—"sprawling, really"—on the floor with her back against the sofa.

"And, she seemed to have passed out, Inspector. Gone to sleep, anyway. Only—well, it didn't seem right, you know. That awful bruise on her head and this sudden unconsciousness. Well, it frightened me. I'm a nurse, you know. Used to be, anyway. In New York. At Saint Vincent's for years. Then at Doctors Hospital. I'm retired now, of course. But I haven't forgotten my training. And—well, it looked to me as if it might be concussion. So, I tried to call somebody. Only the phone was dead. The way it is now."

"Yes, Mrs. Cummins. Pulled loose from the wall. You didn't notice that?"

"Not right away. I was too upset. Too worried about her. And—well, I didn't know what to do. Which isn't really like me at all, you know. I wanted to get help, but the phone was dead. And I was afraid to leave her and go somewhere for help. And I had some people coming. Bringing a female for the Prince. They're almost due now, actually. I thought they could get somebody to help. But you came instead. Only it's taking the ambulance a long time to get here, isn't it?"

"Yes, it does seem to be, Mrs. Cummins. It does, some—"

The sound of a car door slamming shut interrupted him. It didn't however, sound like an ambulance door. Too light a sound for that.

"There it is, finally," Grace Cummins said. "I'll go."

Her smock brushed against Heimrich as she went. The swinging garment swished against his hip. Whatever was in the pocket was small. Small and hard.

Heimrich could hear a door opening; he could hear her inquiring, "Yes?" He could not distinguish the words of the answer, only the much lower sound of a male voice. "Why yes, Doctor," Grace Cummins said. "As a matter of fact, he is."

Her heels clicked on the wooden floor of the entrance hall. The footfalls behind her were heavier, softer. Dr. Latham Rorke was, apparently, wearing soft-soled shoes, suitable for hospital corridors. Mrs. Cummins appeared in the living-room doorway and started a sentence. "It's Dr.—"

She did not finish because Latham Rorke spoke from behind her. He said, "Inspector, Mrs. Heimrich said—" He did not finish either. He saw the girl on the sofa. He said, *"Jesus!"* and went toward her.

"Yes, Doctor," Heimrich said. "A patient for you, I'm afraid." But by that time Rorke was on his knees beside the sleeping girl. His hand was feeling her wrist for the pulse. He did not time it. After a second or two, he gently pushed up her eyelids and looked into her eyes. Then he put his head down on her chest and listened. Then he stood up and looked down at her.

"She's very sound asleep, Doctor," Mrs. Cummins said. "It came over her very suddenly. I'm afraid she's concussed, doctor. I've seen this sort of thing in emergency wards. All right one minute. Out cold the next. I used to be a nurse, you know."

164

Rorke did not appear to hear her. He faced Heimrich.

"How did she get here, Inspector?" he said. There seemed to be accusation in his voice. But perhaps it was only shock.

"According to Mrs. Cummins," Heimrich said, "she just walked in this morning. Said something about people being after her. Mrs. Cummins gave her a cup of coffee because she seemed to need something, Mrs. Cummins thought. She drank the first cup and Mrs. Cummins went to get her another. And came back to find her on the floor, asleep."

"Hell," Rorke said, "she's not just asleep. Anybody can see that. Aftermath of a concussion, could be. Or—"

"Yes, Doctor," Heimrich said. "Probably the concussion, as Nurse Cummins says. An ambulance is on its way."

"Just this morning, Inspector? When she came here, I mean? But it was Sunday night she—"

"Yes, Doctor. There are a good many missing hours. But it was just this morning. What we're told, anyway."

There was nothing special in Heimrich's voice as he said this; nothing to make Latham Rorke look at him searchingly and then, for a moment, at Mrs. Grace Cummins, R.N. He did seem about to say something, but again there was the thud of a closing car door outside. And again Mrs. Cummins went to the house door. There did not, this time, appear to be anything heavy in her smock pocket. The smock swung lightly around the stocky woman.

"Why, Mrs. Jenkins," the cattery owner said. "If you'll bring her this way. It's all set up."

She was answered by a scream, not human but apparently anguished.

"There, baby." Another female voice, presumably that of Mrs. Jenkins. "It's going to be all right."

The wailing Siamese cat did not appear to think so. It, almost certainly the expected "she," screamed again, in greater anguish than ever.

"Female in season," Rorke said. "They make a hell of a noise, don't they? 'Calling,' they call it. Where's that damn ambulance?"

He was answered by the distant sound of a siren. It sounded again, not so distantly.

"As you hear," Heimrich said.

There were again footfalls from the entrance hall of the big white house. This time there were two pairs of clicking heels. They did not approach the living-room door, but their sounds diminished. The cat, undoubtedly imprisoned in a carrying case, screamed again.

"Brought to be serviced," Heimrich said. "Mated. Whatever they call it. By Prince Ling Tau, the cat of cats. Which will be quite a trick, considering." He did not say considering what. Latham Rorke was again on his knees beside Carol Arnold. Again he was taking her pulse. This time he was reading his watch as he counted the pulsing in the wrist he held.

"She'll be all right, Doctor," Heimrich said. Rorke did not respond to this comforting—and clearly unfounded—assurance.

The siren sounded again, very close this time. Turning off the highway, almost certainly. Heimrich went to the door to meet it; to guide the attendants.

They wheeled the stretcher in and lifted Carol Arnold onto it. "Same kid as last time," one of them said to the other as they lifted the stretcher into the ambulance. "Same one we picked up Sunday, remember? An out-of-luck girl, seems like."

Rorke climbed into the ambulance with his girl, his out-of-luck girl. Yes, he would call the barracks when she was able to talk.

"When they bring her out of it," he told Inspector Heimrich. "You know it's not the concussion, don't you?"

"Only a guess, Doctor. A layman's guess. An overdose, you think?"

"I'm pretty damn—" Rorke said, but then one of the attendants closed the ambulance doors, shutting him into silence.

12

Heimrich used the Buick's telephone and got Lieutenant Forniss on it. Did Forniss, by any chance, know anyone in New York who was connected with the nursing profession?

Well, as a matter of fact, Forniss did. At any rate, he had. An Eleanor Lipscomb. That was, she had been Eleanor Lipscomb. Probably Eleanor something else by now. Not a girl likely to have stayed unmarried all these years since Korea. Perhaps not even stayed a nurse, although the last he'd heard, she had. Supervisor of nurses at some New York hospital, a couple of years ago, anyhow. "She was a Navy nurse, M.L. On a hospital ship. A j.g., way I remember it. Nice-looking girl. I dated her a couple of times back then. In San Francisco, that was. We were both on terminal leave. Why, M.L.?"

Heimrich told him why. In regard to Grace Cummins, R.N. Anything he could get, by telephone. Through the former lieutenant, junior grade, if he could get in touch with her. Otherwise through the New York Police Department, which probably wouldn't have anything.

"She says she was on the nursing staff at Saint Vincent's, Charley. Some time ago, probably. At Doctors later, she says. Just background, Charley."

Charles Forniss said, "Yep," and was M.L. coming in?

"Later, probably." Heimrich looked at his watch. A few minutes after eleven.

"Tell you what, Charley. I'll probably be at the inn around—oh, make it one o'clock. Try me there."

Forniss would do.

Heimrich called Susan. Yes, she'd get a cab down and join him at the Old Stone Inn for lunch. Any special reason? "Just lunch, dear. And how's the pooch?"

Colonel seemed to be all right, although not especially ambitious. No desire to go out and frolic in the sunshine. Taking advantage of the air conditioning. "Around twelve thirty, dear?"

Heimrich thought so. He had to stop by Cold Harbor first. In the bar, of course. Susan said, "Of course, Merton dear," with almost no amusement in her voice.

Heimrich drove to Cold Harbor. The local police told him where he might find the First Baptist Church. It was a couple of miles out on Crescent Street, which was to the right, two blocks down that way.

Crescent Street turned out to be a perfectly straight street, which did not much surprise Merton Heimrich. Probably fifty years ago, or a hundred years ago, it had curved in a crescent. Straightening it had not changed its name.

169

The First Baptist Church of Cold Harbor might well have stood a hundred years ago as it stood now —white and with a steeple, and sedate. A very pretty little church, actually, and in the tradition of New England. New England has a tendency to creep into New York by osmosis.

The First Baptist Church had its own graveyard. It also had a locked front door. But an elderly man was pushing a lawn mower among the gravestones. Did he know where Dr. James might be found?

"You meaning the Rev James, mister? He ain't no doctor I ever heard of."

"The Reverend Mr. James then," Heimrich said.

He could try the parsonage. Just up the road a piece. Only the Rev might be out, making what he called his calls. Heimrich thanked the church's yard-man—or sexton; did Baptists run to sextons?—and drove the piece up the road, as indicated. The parson-age was white as the church was, although not so recently painted. A girl of about four was tangled with a small white dog in the front yard. She untangled herself from the leash, and the dog barked at Heim-rich, although not with malice.

"Is your father at home, baby?"

"Yes. But I'm not a baby, mister. Babies are like that." She held her hands about a foot apart.

"Of course," Heimrich said.

A slight young woman in a large apron appeared on the front porch.

"That's Mamma," the little girl said. "Come here, Benjamin." She tugged at Benjamin's lead and the little dog jumped against her, not quite knocking her over.

"*Benjy!*" the young woman in the excessive apron said. "Quit that! You're a *bad* dog!"

The small white dog paid no attention. He did not

quit his enthusiastic bouncing against the little girl, who showed no evidence of wanting him to. Heimrich said, "Mrs. James?" and, when she nodded her head, "I wonder if I might see your husband, if he's in?"

"Of course," she said. "He's in his study. Working on Sunday's sermon. Is it church business?"

"In a way," Heimrich told her. "I won't interrupt him for long, Mrs. James."

He followed her into the small white house, past old and rather bored furniture of assorted styles. She knocked on a closed door. She said, "There's somebody to see you, dear. He says it's church business."

Well, Heimrich thought, I did say that. And she didn't say he was in his "den."

She opened the door and said, "Go right on in. He never hears me when he's working."

Heimrich went into a very small room. The man in it was in his early or mid- thirties. He was wearing tennis shorts and a tennis shirt. He did not, to Heimrich, look especially like a clergyman or, for that matter, a Baptist, born again or not. But Merton Heimrich, born Episcopalian but no longer working at it, knows few Baptists. He is also quite willing to settle for the one the country has. Which makes him a little singular in Van Brunt.

The man dressed for tennis was sitting in front of a portable typewriter. There was a blank sheet of paper in the typewriter, and the Reverend Mr. James was staring at it. Heimrich cleared his throat.

"Yes," James said. "I heard her." He turned to face Heimrich, who, more or less involuntarily, said, "Doctor." He managed to avoid saying "Father." The church of his boyhood had been high.

"Just mister," James said. "Not a doctor of divinity. Regarding church business, my wife said."

"In a way. About one of your church members, anyway. I'm a policeman, by the way."

James stood up at that. He regarded Heimrich for several seconds. Standing, James looked more than ever like an athlete.

"I doubt if any member of our church has broken the law," James said. "And you aren't in uniform, are you?"

"It's not about lawbreaking," Heimrich said. "And you're not in uniform either, are you, Reverend?"

James laughed at that. He had a friendly laugh.

"I get edgy when I'm trying to think out a sermon," James said. "God's words don't come easily. To me, anyway. You're a detective, I suppose. Captain, or something?"

"Inspector, Mr. James. Inspector Heimrich."

"Yes, Inspector. I've heard of you, haven't I?"

"Possibly. I live just down the road in Van Brunt."

"And your stepson is the tennis pro at the club," James said. "Friend of mine's a member. Taken me along once or twice. What member of our church, Inspector? And what about him or her?"

"Mrs. Grace Cummins. And was she at church last Sunday? The noon service?"

"Dear Mrs. Cummins," James said. "Yes, I'm sure she was, Inspector. She is very faithful. She almost never misses a service. Usually sits up front, too. Not like many of my—er—flock. Yes, I'm quite sure she attended service last Sunday. Why, Inspector?"

"Just checking up on things," Heimrich said. "Quite sure, Mr. James? Only quite? She says she did attend the noon service."

"Then she did," James said. "Do you question her statement?"

172

"In my line of work, we question a great many things, Mr. James. Seek corroboration, anyway. I'm afraid we're not long on faith. As men of the cloth are, of course."

Heimrich had picked his descriptive phrase out, he supposed, of his boyhood. It did not, under these circumstances, seem particularly appropriate. "It may be important," he told the young clergyman dressed for tennis. "Have you a specific memory that Mrs. Cummins was at church Sunday? Or is it—well, just that you assume she was because she almost always is?"

James stood for a moment and looked at Heimrich. Then he turned away and moved to a window. It was a small window and his body blocked it, and blocked out what little air stirred through it into the small, hot room. The parsonage, which Heimrich managed not to think of as the rectory, did not run to air conditioning.

James looked out the window for several minutes. When he turned back, his young face seemed troubled.

"As near as I can come to it," he said, "I can't remember her *not* being at the service. I think I would if she hadn't been. She's—well, she's pretty much a fixture, if you know what I mean. What it comes to, I'm sure she must have been. In her usual pew. I'm almost certain I'd have noticed if her pew had been empty."

"Only almost, Mr. James?"

"I'm afraid so, Inspector. You see, after the services, I go to the church door to tell the worshipers good-bye. Most of us do. The pastors of churches as small as mine, anyway. I've been trying to visualize last Sunday. The members I said good-bye to. And, well, I can't visualize Mrs. Cummins. She always tells me how good and inspiring my sermon was. Whether it was or not. I can't remember her doing that last Sunday. But I'm almost sure she did."

"But it's still almost, isn't it?"

"I'm afraid so, Inspector. Not good enough, I suppose? But if she said she was at the service—well, I'm sure she's a truthful woman. I know she's a devout one. What we'd call a true believer, of the old tradition, actually. A woman of deep faith, unquestioning faith. People like that do not tell untruths, Inspector."

A "man of the cloth," even if in tennis shorts. A man of simple faith. But it was not a faith Heimrich, or any policeman, could hold. Even the righteous can sometimes lie, if the cause is good enough.

"Not what you came for, is it?" James said. "I'm sorry, Inspector."

"No, Mr. James. Not quite. But I'm glad to get your opinion of Mrs. Cummins. A truthful woman. A deeply religious one, you think. A believer in what people call the old-time religion."

"Certainly. As I am. Oh, with some reservations, I suppose. A little more tolerant of allegory than old-timers like Mrs. Cummins, possibly. But not as to the essential truth, which I think manifest. You are a Christian, Inspector?"

"By birth," Heimrich said. "Not devout, I'm afraid. I don't really believe a whale swallowed Jonah and—well, spit him up again. Mrs. Cummins does, I assume."

"And in a literal hell and a literal heaven," James said. "And probably that God has a beard."

"And in an eye for an eye and a tooth for a tooth?"

"Probably, Inspector. The faith of her fathers, certainly. As do I. With, possibly, a few reservations. Not toward the essentials. I wouldn't have you think that. Do you happen to be a Catholic, Inspector?"

174

It was an entirely unexpected question.

"Not of the Roman variety," Heimrich said. "The priest of the church my parents took me to as a boy was careful to make that distinction. He also preferred to be addressed as 'Father.' Well—thank you, Mr. James."

"For very little, I'm afraid. God bless you, Inspector."

Both the little girl and the little dog were gone when Heimrich left the parsonage. Probably, he thought, they were both having lunch. It was still a little early for his own. He drove slowly down to Van Brunt and the Old Stone Inn.

It was only twenty after twelve when Heimrich went into the inn through the door which led directly to what the inn prefers to think of as the "taproom." But Susan was already there. She was sitting, unexpectedly, with Lieutenant Charles Forniss, New York State Police.

Heimrich joined them. Neither had a drink, but the barman was mixing. When Heimrich came in, the barman looked across the cool room at him, and Heimrich nodded. The barman added a jigger of gin and a flick of vermouth to his mixing glass and resumed stirring. Then he scooped ice into a cocktail glass and put it beside another glass, also filled with ice, in front of him on the bar.

Heimrich said, "Hi, dear," to Susan. He raised his eyebrows toward Charles Forniss. Forniss smiled and, slowly, shook his head.

"Nothing hot," Forniss said. "Just felt like getting away from the barracks. The air conditioning's on the blink again."

The barman brought their drinks. Forniss's was bourbon on the rocks. The barman said, "Morning,

Mrs. Heimrich. Inspector." Heimrich said, "Morning," having, once more, forgotten the barman's name. Susan smiled at the barman.

Heimrich raised his eyebrows again toward Forniss.

"Miss Lipscomb's still supervisor of nurses at Saint Vincent's. Not Miss Lipscomb any more. Mrs. Larkin now. But she remembered me. On the third try. She also remembered Mrs. Cummins. As Grace Clarke, but the same gal. She was on the staff at the hospital. Left and went to Doctors just as Eleanor was coming on the St. Vincent's staff. But Eleanor kept hearing about her, she says. Gossip about her. Seems there was quite a bit of that."

Eleanor Larkin, née Lipscomb, had given Forniss the name of the nurses' supervisor at Doctors Hospital. "A Miss Klein." Miss Klein had said all that was twenty years ago, and why on earth? She had been told it was merely a routine inquiry and had said, "Huh!" but had not seen any reason why not.

Yes, Grace Clarke had been a nurse at the hospital. A surgical nurse at first. Then a private nurse, her name on the list of those available for private duty. "Before my time, actually," Nurse Klein had told Forniss. Nurse Clarke had then been in her middle thirties, at Nurse Klein's guess.

It wouldn't have been Heimrich's guess, thinking of the stocky, dominating woman who now ministered to cats instead of humans; who was a devout, and apparently fundamentalist, Baptist. Middle forties, twenty years ago, would have been Merton Heimrich's guess. However—

"So, M.L., Miss Clarke married one of her patients. A Randolph Cummins. A good deal older than she, apparently. Somewhere in his sixties, Nurse

Klein thinks. But it's all something she's just heard about. A nurse who, well, hit it big. Something nurses think about happening, since sometimes it does. Marry a rich man who is grateful to you, indebted to you, and wants—well, to take you home with him. Way it worked out for Miss Clarke, anyway."

About then, Nurse Klein had begun to freeze up. She had pointed out that nurses, like doctors, have their code and that she shouldn't be repeating gossip about former patients at her hospital. Even if they had not been her patients.

But Forniss, like all good detectives, can be persuasive on occasion. Well, he must remember it was all gossip. Probably no truth in it. Just a story going around.

The story was that Randolph Cummins had been a cardiac patient and had left the hospital under strict recommendations as to his activities for the rest of his life, if he expected to have much rest left to it. Very circumscribed activities, they would have to be. No violent exercise, of course. Getting out of bed in the mornings very slowly, one movement at a time. Walking slowly, and resting at the first feeling of fatigue. "The usual things, Lieutenant. No sexual activity, of course."

"What his doctor told him?" Forniss had asked and, jumping ahead, had asked the name of the doctor. The doctor had been named Koenig. Alexander Koenig. Only he was dead now; had died, actually, a year or so before Cummins died, which had been about three years after his marriage. The way Miss Klein got it, but it was merely the story going around. The lieutenant must understand that. And probably she had talked too much already. Forniss had told her that the police protect their sources.

Well, the story, for what it was worth, was that Randolph Cummins had died very suddenly, apparently while engaged in the sexual activity which had been forbidden him. And because Dr. Koenig was dead, and no other doctor had treated him recently, the question of a death certificate had come up. Which, as the lieutenant probably knew, meant the medical examiner and an autopsy.

"But that just proved it had been his heart, as everyone had known, Lieutenant."

"You check with the M.E.'s office, Charley?"

Charley had not. They could if they decided it was necessary. But one other thing Nurse Klein had told him, as, remember, only gossip. Randolph Cummins had not been as rich as everyone supposed he was. Nobody knew how much Grace Cummins had inherited, but the prevailing guess had been not more than fifty thousand dollars.

"About enough to set her up in the cat-breeding business," Heimrich said. "Twenty years or so ago, she might have got the house for twenty. I've no idea what beginning cats would have cost her."

Neither had Charles Forniss. Neither had Susan.

"Although," Susan said, "I wouldn't think there was all that much money in breeding cats. Even very pedigreed cats."

Merton Heimrich wouldn't have thought so, either. Still, a stud fee of two hundred dollars might well add up.

"Depending," Susan said, "on the durability of the tomcat."

Heimrich said no to a second drink, and so, after a quick glance at him, did Susan. Forniss, after a thoughtful moment, joined them in abstention. A waitress came from the main dining room, and they ordered. They had finished lunch and were drinking coffee when the bar telephone rang. The barman answered it and then held up the receiver. He said, "For you, Inspector."

Heimrich took his last swallow. He crossed the room to the telephone. He spoke his name into it. He said, "Yes, Doctor," to Latham Rorke, M.D. He said, "Yes, we do leave word where we'll be."

Miss Carol Arnold had regained consciousness. Yes, an overdose of a barbiturate had caused her to lose it. A resident at the Cold Harbor Hospital had confirmed that. She would be all right. They had caught her in time.

"Just in time," Rorke said, with bitterness as well as relief in his voice. "She's willing to talk to you, and the resident says she can. For a few minutes, anyway. And, well, she's his patient. So I guess what I think doesn't matter."

"We'll make it as easy for her as we can, Doctor," Heimrich promised. "We'll be along in half an hour or so. Yes, I'll be bringing another officer with me. Oh, because two memories can be better than one. Yes, I'd expect you to, Doctor."

"We can talk to Miss Arnold now," Heimrich told Forniss, back at their table. "Her doctor thinks it will be all right. Rorke doesn't, and wants to be with us when we talk to her."

"And holding her hand," Susan said. "I can't say I blame him. The two of you are so big and she's so little."

They would drop Susan off at home. They would use both cars. Neither the Buick nor the car Forniss had driven down from the barracks was marked as a police vehicle.

It was a little more than half an hour before they

179

reached the hospital. They had had, briefly, to commune with Colonel, who had been sitting at the door of the house when they reached it. He had looked very neglected, and his woof had been reproachful. But it often was, particularly when everybody went away and left him. Mite had stepped out—through the feline exit.

Carol Arnold was in the room she had been in before. Rorke was sitting by her bed. He was not actually holding her hand. A nurse was doing that, taking her pulse. "We're doing very well indeed, aren't we, dear?" the nurse said. "Only we do need rest, don't we?"

Carol was very pale, her eyes were very large. She did not audibly concur in the nurse's estimate of their condition. She did say, "Hi, Inspector." Her voice was very small.

The room was large enough so that Forniss could sit several feet from the bed. He got out a notebook.

13

"Do you feel up to a few questions, Miss Arnold?" Heimrich said. "We'll try not to make them too many."

She raised her voice a little when she answered. It was, Heimrich thought, an effort for her to raise her voice.

"Tired," she said. "And I guess a little woozy. But all right, really. What do you want to ask me, Inspector?"

"Anything you can tell us about this morning. About going to Mrs. Cummins's place."

Her eyes seemed to grow even larger. She moved her head from side to side on the pillows which propped it.

She said, "This morning? I don't seem to remember this morning much. I said I'm woozy. Oh, something about the telephone and trying to call Lathe at the hospital. Not this hospital. The one at White Plains. Only I didn't get him. Something happened. I don't seem to remember what. Wasn't I cut off, or something?"

"Yes," Heimrich said. "I meant, going to Mrs. Cummins's place this morning. Asking her to take you in because somebody was after you. Because 'they' were trying to find you. Wasn't it that way? Quite early this morning?"

"You've got it wrong, Inspector. I went there last night. After Lathe took me back to Dr. Barton's hospital. When I got to worrying about the poor little cat. The one she calls Lady Bella. The one I—I was taking to her as she asked me to. Last night I went there. Wasn't it last night?"

Heimrich shook his head.

"No, Miss Arnold. It must have been night before last—Sunday evening. That was when Dr. Rorke drove you back from here. You had been brought here, you remember, because the car you were driving Sunday morning ran into a tree. Today is Tuesday, Miss Arnold."

She turned her head on the pillows and looked at Latham Rorke. He said, "Yes, dear. It was night before last, not last night." Then he said, "She's not up to this, Inspector. Can't you see that?"

"Perhaps you're—" Heimrich said, but the girl interrupted him. Her voice seemed to be stronger.

"No," she said. "I want to get things straightened out. So they're not all muddled. Maybe it wasn't last night. Maybe it was Sunday night. Anyway, it was a couple of hours after Lathe got me to the Bartons'. I had a headache. I remember that. I'd bumped my head somehow. Hadn't I?"

"Yes, Miss Arnold. In the car accident. That evening. Do you remember that evening?"

"Of course. It was Sunday morning she called and

182

asked if I'd bring Lady Bella over. So I borrowed the Pontiac and put the little cat in a case and drove over and—and had that accident. The carrying case was on the seat beside me with the cat in it. I told you that before, didn't I?"

"Yes, Miss Arnold. Only—"

"Nobody had told me what happened to Lady Bella. I—well, I kept thinking maybe she'd been hurt in the accident. Killed, even. So, I was worried. And my head ached. I went into Dr. Barton's office bedroom and lay down, while I was trying to think what to do. But I was too worried to stay there. I thought maybe Mrs. Cummins had gone down to the car—the one I smashed up—and carried the little cat back home. So, well, I borrowed Mrs. Evans's car and drove over to see."

"Yes. You went to the cattery. Then?"

"She came to the door. She had a glass in her hand. I said, 'Is Lady Bella all right?' And she said, 'Of course, dear,' and how had I bumped my head? I told her what had happened, and she was—oh, very sympathetic and insisted I come in and sit down, and that I needed a drink and that she'd get me one. And, well, I was feeling pretty pooped and it seemed like a good idea, and she brought me a drink. And I drank it and—"

The girl closed her eyes. "I guess I'm really very tired," she said, and the voice was small again.

"Too tired, Inspector," Rorke said, and his voice was strong and hard. "You can't go on with this."

Carol opened her eyes again and turned her head toward Latham Rorke. She said, "Please, dear. I've got to get things straight. Where was I, Inspector?"

"Mrs. Cummins said the cat was all right, and that you needed a drink. And she got you one. All

183

right, Doctor. I've almost finished bothering Miss Arnold. After you finished the drink, Miss Arnold? Then?"

"I was still worried about the little cat. I think I asked Mrs. Cummins if I could see Lady Bella. Just so I wouldn't be so worried. Feel so guilty about her. And she said, 'Of course,' and took me to the place where she keeps the cats. There's a section built onto the house—"

"Yes, Miss Arnold. I know the setup there. She showed you this Lady Bella. She's a rather small sealpoint Siamese, isn't she?"

"Yes. Most female Siamese cats are small."

"You knew it was the right cat? The one you had been taking back when this accident happened? I mean, they must all look pretty much alike. Same markings, I gather?"

"Yes. All seal points do look pretty much alike. Clear markings, pointed faces—if they're show cats, that is. Long tails, with no kink in them. There used to be kinks, but they've been breeding that out for generations. Cat generations, I mean. And no crossed eyes, of course. Most of them used to have crossed eyes, they say. The kink and the crossed eyes used not to matter. To people who show cats. I don't know that either thing ever mattered much to the cats. Except for lack of depth perception, of course. From the crossed eyes, that is."

"Yes, Miss Arnold."

"Anyway, a cross-eyed Siamese hasn't a chance of winning a ribbon nowadays. Or cats with tabby markings on their back legs. Or with round faces. Cat judges are very particular about such things. And they are recessive characteristics in Siamese cats. But being Siamese is recessive too, of course. I'm giving a lecture

184

about cats, aren't I? You should hear me on horses."

"It's very interesting, Miss Arnold," Heimrich said, with some insincerity. "You did make sure the cat Mrs. Cummins showed you was Lady Bella?"

"I spoke to her. By name. And she answered. They're great talkers, you know."

"You made sure about the cat, Miss Arnold. And then?"

She raised herself against the pillows and looked at him with very wide eyes.

"Then it just stops, Inspector. The whole thing just stops. It's absurd, really. But then I was here. It couldn't have been as long ago as Sunday. It *couldn't* have been."

Rorke stood up then. He said, "That's enough, Heimrich. More than enough. And I *am* a doctor."

Heimrich stood up. Forniss put away the notebook he'd been jotting in and stood up too. Rorke did not stand up. He reached out a hand and took one of Carol's, which was given him readily. Rorke leaned toward the girl and spoke softly. Heimrich did not hear what he said, or try to.

At the door, Heimrich stopped to let the nurse in. She smiled brightly. "We're doing just fine, aren't we?" the nurse said. "We're going to be perfectly all right very soon now, aren't we?"

Heimrich said he was sure they were, and he and Forniss went down to their cars. At Heimrich's they stopped.

"Well, M.L.," Forniss said, "we certainly know a good deal about Siamese cats, don't we? More than we need to know, seems to me."

"Could be, Charley. Still, Siamese cats are pretty much in the middle of things, aren't they? One Siamese cat, anyway."

185

"O.K., M.L. And I'll get along back to the barracks."

Heimrich shook his head. "Not yet, I think," he said. "We'll have your car picked up. I'd like you to come along with me. To a cattery, Charley."

Forniss, who somewhat prefers dogs but is not rabid about it, said "Jesus!" But he got into the Buick.

"Discrepancies, Charley," Heimrich said as he started the Buick rolling out of the hospital parking lot. On their way to the Linwood Cattery he filled Charles Forniss in. What it came to, Forniss agreed, you can't believe anybody. Not if you're a cop.

Mrs. Grace Cummins, R.N., was sitting on the front porch of the white house which was the Linwood Cattery when Heimrich and Forniss reached it. She still wore the pants suit with the smock over it. The costume looked warm for so hot a day, but the porch was shaded. She stood up when the Buick stopped in front of the house. She looked at the Buick and then sat down again. If she had been waiting for something, it was evidently not the police.

"I thought you were the man about the telephone," she said as the two large policemen got out of the car. "They never come when you need them, do they? And I'm cut off from—from everything. You did call the repair department, didn't you?"

"Yes, Mrs. Cummins. They'll be along."

"And," Mrs. Cummins said, "I did want to call the hospital and see how that poor child is. I'm worried about her. Concussion can be such a tricky thing, you know. Or perhaps you don't. Not the way I do. Not the way a nurse does."

"Miss Arnold seems to be doing very well," Heimrich said. "She's regained consciousness. But she's still a little confused about things."

186

The stocky woman nodded her head.

"The poor child," she said. "It happens that way so often with concussion. Sometimes they never do get things straight afterward, you know. There's always a blank space left for some of them."

"Yes," Heimrich said, "I do understand, nurse. Miss Arnold is still worried about that little cat of yours. Lady Bella. The one she still seems to think was in the car with her when she ran into the tree. While you were at church last Sunday."

"The poor, poor child. But I told her Lady Bella was all right. That I'd brought her home from Dr. Barton's when I brought the other one. The one he'd operated on."

"I know," Heimrich said. "But she's still confused and worried about—the cat you call Lady Bella."

"Her call name, Inspector. The name they answer to. Think of themselves as, I suppose. Their registered names—well, they're sometimes too long for a cat to remember."

Heimrich said he saw.

"The thing is," he said, "Miss Arnold still isn't sure. Confused, as you say. She asked me to—well, come here and have a look at Lady Bella. I promised her I would. So, I'd like to, Mrs. Cummins. Take the worry off her mind. Will it be all right if I have a look?"

"Well," the stocky woman said, "I suppose so. If you can't take my word for it. If you think it's a load on the poor child's mind."

"It's not a question of not taking your word, Mrs. Cummins. But it is on her mind. Very much on her mind, I'm afraid. And I did promise I'd look at the little cat."

187

"All right," Mrs. Cummins said. "Although I don't really see what good it will do her. All purebred Siamese cats look pretty much alike to an outsider. I mean to a person who doesn't know anything about them. And if they're not purebred, they don't look like Siamese cats at all, of course. But come on."

She led the way into the house. Heimrich went after her. Inside the door, Forniss said, "M.L.?"

"Yes, Charley, I think so," Heimrich said. So both tall detectives followed Grace Cummins down a long corridor and then, when she opened it for them, through a door on the left.

The corridor floor they had walked on had creaked a little under their feet, the protesting whines of an old frame house. The room they went into was different. The carpeted floor was firm under their feet; there was a neutral grass-cloth covering on the walls. It was cooler than the rest of the house had been.

It was an oblong room, thirty feet or more long; half as wide. Along the walls on either side, at floor level, there were enclosures, faced by wire-mesh doors. There were five such pens along either wall, and there were cats in eight of the pens, which were too ample to be called cages. Three of the cats were curled in cushioned beds in their quarters; each pen had a litter pan, and there were pans of water in all the occupied pens.

"Here's Bella," Mrs. Cummins said, and stopped in front of one of the pens.

Lady Bella had been resting in her bed, but apparently not asleep. When Mrs. Cummins said her call name, the little cat got out of bed and came to the front of the pen. She said something which sounded like "Mow-ow?" in a not loud, but inquiring voice. Mrs. Cummins said, "Pretty girl," and spoke in a softer voice than Heimrich had heard her use before.

Her small ladyship did, as Mrs. Cummins had assured them she would, look like a seal-point Siamese cat—looked like the cats in the pens on either side of hers. She was slender, and rather long for her size; her crisply pointed ears were dark brown, as was part of her face. Tracings of brown ran from her mask to the ears. Her brown tail was longer than one would have expected and rather like a whip. Her body was a pale cream color, except for brown leggings on all four legs.

Her eyes, slitted against the light, were vividly blue.

"So there you are," said Mrs. Cummins. "You can tell Miss Arnold she's all right, can't you? Imagine her being so worried!"

"She's a very pretty cat," Heimrich said. "Lady Bella, that is. Yes, Miss Arnold will be relieved."

Relieved that he had seen a dainty young Siamese female who had been identified to him as Lady Bella, and who had, for what it was worth, answered to her call name. And who, as she had turned her back to them and walked toward her bed, had proven herself female. So—Lady Bella was home safe and evidently enjoying being there. How she got there was, of course, another matter. Been brought home, in a carrying box with another cat, as her owner said? Or had somehow got out of another case in a damaged car and trotted the quarter of a mile to the cattery? And, at the door, spoken to be let in?

Probably, of course, the former. Cat boxes are not designed to be opened from inside by their occupants.

"She's very good," Mrs. Cummins said. "More than just pretty, Inspector. We're going to win us a lot of ribbons, aren't we, Bella?"

Lady Bella did not respond to this, probably thinking it too obvious to need rejoinder.

"So there you are," Mrs. Cummins said again. "Is there something else you want, Inspector?"

"Well," Heimrich said, "I don't think so, do you, Charley?"

Charley Forniss said, "Mmm," not knowing which way the cat—or the inspector—was going to jump.

"While we're here," Heimrich said, "I'd rather like to see this famous cat of yours, Mrs. Cummins. This best cat of last year. Prince Tau Ling, isn't it?"

"Ling Tau," Mrs. Cummins said. "All right. But he'll just look like another Siamese cat to you, probably. Only judges would know the difference. And us breeders, of course. Come along, then."

She walked down the room. At the end of it were two much larger pens, side by side. Each of these had a contraption at the wall which Heimrich recognized as a cat door. They were like the one Mite had at home and used when he chose, although he much preferred to have people open doors for him. Cats expect service from their captive humans.

Only one of the big pens was occupied. It was also hung with ribbons, which were topped by a rosette of ribbon. There were a dozen such ribbons, most of them blue, but one golden.

The cat whose dwelling was thus adorned looked, from in front, very much like Lady Bella. But he was much larger. He was, Heimrich thought and said, a very handsome cat.

"That's putting it mildly, isn't it, Princy?" Mrs. Cummins said.

Prince Ling Tau, who had come to the front of his residence to inspect visitors, made no comment. He looked up at Heimrich through slitted and very blue eyes, set slanting in his head. An Oriental slant, most evident with the pupils narrowed. And evident, too,

190

was the fact that Prince Ling Tau was, although only slightly, cross-eyed.

Hence, if Carol Arnold was to be believed, which Heimrich had no special reason to doubt, not likely to be adjudged the best Siamese cat of last year, or of any year. Hence, not Prince Ling Tau, as advertised—as rather extensively advertised.

"He looks very healthy," Heimrich said. "Quite recovered from whatever was the matter with him last January."

"January, Inspector?"

"When he was in Dr. Barton's hospital. Being treated for whatever was the matter with him."

"Oh, that," Mrs. Cummins said. "It wasn't anything, really. Barton thought he might have lung congestion, which they get sometimes. But he didn't have, fortunately. Just a slight cold. He was only there a couple of days. He's been fine ever since."

"Earning his board and keep, I gather," Heimrich said.

Grace Cummins raised heavy eyebrows.

"At two hundred dollars a mating," Heimrich said. "A servicing. Whatever you call it. Quite capable of that, evidently. How many times since last January, Mrs. Cummins? Just roughly?"

"I'd have to look at my records to tell you that. My certifications to the owners of the queens. To be part of the papers when they registered the kittens with the CFA. The Cat Fanciers Association, that is. Where the Prince is registered."

"Rather like the Jockey Club for horses, I gather," Heimrich said. "Or the Kennel Club for dogs."

"Pretty much, Inspector. But there are other associations which register cats. Sponsor shows, you know. Or their member clubs do."

"Yes," Heimrich said. "I'm beginning to under-

stand. You know what a ringer is, Mrs. Cummins?"
She repeated the word, with a rising inflection.

"In racing terminology," Heimrich said, "a horse
running under another horse's registered name.
When something happens to the entered horse. Or his
trainer decides he isn't running well. A substitute
horse, who looks enough like the entered horse to pass.
It's fraud, of course. Unpopular with the Jockey Club.
And with the law. How many times has Prince served
at stud, Mrs. Cummins? From January on? Once a
week? Or oftener?"

"I told you I'd have to look—"

"Yes, Mrs. Cummins. You said you'd have to look
it up. At two hundred dollars a time. A very high stud
fee, I'm told."

"For the grand champion of grand champions? I
don't think so. And other breeders apparently don't.
We get more applications than we can handle, Inspector. And we select the females very carefully. The
owners have to send me copies of the papers, of course.
To breed potential grand champions, like Princy
here."

Princy continued to look up at Heimrich rather
than at his owner, although she had used his call name.

"To be mated with the best cat of last year. The
all-American cat. Although this cat isn't he. Prince
Ling Tau died last January at the animal hospital,
didn't he? Although you've been advertising him as at
stud ever since. Did you think Dr. Barton killed Ling
Tau, Mrs. Cummins? Is that why you killed Barton?
An eye for an eye and a tooth for a tooth, Mrs. Cummins? Or—a man for a cat?"

"I don't—" she said and her voice was strangled.
"What are you talking about? You must have gone—"

She did not finish. Heimrich finished for her.

192

"No," he said, "I've not gone mad, Mrs. Cummins. Because, you see, this very handsome cat is cross-eyed. It's a recessive trait in Siamese cats, I'm told. But it keeps them from winning at cat shows. Even as slightly cross-eyed as this cat is, Mrs. Cummins. What is his real name, Mrs. Cummins?"

"Beauty, Inspector. Because he is, isn't he? Aren't you, Beauty?"

The seal point looked at her then. He said, "Wow-ow."

14

IT WAS AFTER SEVEN when Merton Heimrich drove the
Buick between the boulders and up the steep drive to
the house above the Hudson. It was not quite as hot
as it had been. It was only 89 by the door-side ther-
mometer. The sun was getting lower in the west, but
its rays still flooded the terrace. Susan, who had been
warned by telephone from the barracks, was at the
door to welcome him, and to be kissed in return. And
to tell her husband that he looked tired.

"But it is wrapped up, isn't it?" Susan Heimrich
said. "And it is Mrs. Cummins?"

"Not tired," Heimrich said. "Nothing a shower
won't take care of. Yes, dear. Grace Cummins, R.N.
The terrace?"

"It's cooler inside," Susan said. "And less glary.
But we can wear sunglasses."

Heimrich showered while Susan set up the martinis. He was wearing a sports shirt—a tennis shirt,
really—when she brought the tray to the table on the

terrace. He didn't bulge under the shirt. He wasn't, thank heavens, getting breasty, as some big men do. He wore light gray summer slacks, and sunglasses. She put the tray down.

"You smell clean," she said. "As the TV ads assert one ought to. Do all TV commercials have to be vulgar, dear?"

"Apparently it helps," Heimrich said. "Or Madison Avenue thinks it does. Where are our animals?"

"Mite's out somewhere. Colonel's in front of an air-conditioning outlet. But he ate his dinner."

Heimrich poured and stirred and poured again into chilled glasses. They had raised their glasses to click when, softly and with reproach, Colonel woofed from behind the screen door, perversely closed against a dog who wanted to join his family. "He would," Susan said, and went to let the big dog out. Colonel came to Merton to be scratched behind the ears. Then he found a partly shaded area of terrace and thumped down in it. He did not thump any more loudly than usual.

"Does she admit it, Merton?"

"Only in bits and pieces," Heimrich told her. "She knows she's entitled to a lawyer, and she's getting one up from town." (To those who live near the city of New York there is only one "town.") "She denies killing Barton. Arranging for Carol Arnold to have an accident; drugging Carol Sunday night. She says why on earth should she? But she doesn't deny, not specifically, that she's been using a stand-in for Prince Ling Tau. At two hundred a—well, a stand. Knows she can't because any cat show judge would spot the difference. The stand-in, whom she calls Beauty, is cross-eyed. Only a little, but enough to disbar him, apparently. Siamese cats are not allowed to

195

have crossed eyes. Now and then they ignore the rules. As Beauty does. He's a half brother of the Prince, incidentally. Registered with the CFA, as Prince Ling Tau was. Not as Beauty, of course. Some name that's supposed to sound Siamese. Got it down somewhere."

"All right, dear. But you're losing me a little. And we didn't really click. Because of Colonel."

They clicked glasses. They sipped. Briefly, they looked down at the Hudson River, with the sun sparkling on it. Sparkling into their eyes, come to that. But dark glasses helped.

"Why did she kill Dr. Barton?" Susan asked. "And can you prove she did?"

"Because she thinks he killed her prize cat, dear. Who didn't have nine lives. And because Holy Writ approves an eye for an eye and a tooth for a tooth. She's a very religious woman, Susan."

"The Bible also says thou shalt not kill."

"A rule often breached. By nations, by states which prescribe capital punishment. Also by individuals, which leads to the employment of homicide detectives. And, as I said, she thinks Barton killed. Apparently he didn't. Any more than he killed Blake's dog. Not intentionally, anyway. I stopped by the hospital coming down and talked to Miss Arnold."

"She's going to be all right?"

"They're keeping her overnight. But, yes. To be released tomorrow. In Latham Rorke's custody, if he has anything to say about it, and I suspect he will. Anyway, I talked to her on the way home. Dr. Barton had talked to her, as Mrs. Cummins thought he might have. Given her various facts about treating animals, which was part of the reason she was working for him.

196

One of the facts was one I'd never heard of, although he said he could verify it by personal experience—an experience of last winter, he told her. He wasn't much more specific, apparently. But—"

But, Barton had told the pretty girl who was, in a sense, serving as an intern under him, one thing you had to watch out for was an adverse reaction of some animals to barbiturates. In, he had said, one animal in a hundred. Perhaps in two hundred. Barbiturates are used as anesthetics in treating animals. For operations, and for X rays.

"You can't," Heimrich said, "tell a cat or a dog to take a deep breath and hold it, and lie perfectly still. So you give a mild shot of a barbiturate to calm the animal. A quick-acting one like sodium pentothal, usually. In a minute dose."

The chances are a hundred to one, or two hundred or more to one, that the result will be the one wanted. Brief but complete unconsciousness, suitable for the taking of an X-ray photograph.

But, in a tiny number of cases, the reaction may be precisely the opposite. Instead of passing out peacefully, the animal may be stimulated to uncontrollable activity. Even to convulsions. And, if that happens, there's not much to be done about it and the animal may die.

It had happened to Dr. Barton the winter before. He had been about to take chest X rays of a cat who appeared to have congested lungs. The cat had gone into convulsions and died. He had not identified the cat to Carol Arnold. He had also said that similar reactions at rare intervals occurred with humans who were stimulated rather than sedated by barbiturates. Not, so far as Barton knew, thrown into convulsions, but kept alarmingly awake and active.

"This cat who died? It was Mrs. Cummins's prize cat?"

"I'm pretty sure of it. The doctor's records show the cat capital 'D.' I supposed at first the 'D' meant 'discharged.' But it may have meant—probably did mean—'deceased.' ''

"And she killed just for revenge? To avenge her prize cat?"

"The emphasis is on 'prize,' dear. On the pride of the Linwood Cattery. And a cat with a very high stud fee. Probably the financial mainstay of the cattery. And she kept on advertising him as available, although he was dead. And Barton read *The American Cat Fancy*. Saw her advertisements. Saved the copies and—well, brought them to her attention."

"Threatened to expose her?"

"Possibly. Told her to stop her advertising, at the least. Of which the CFA would take a very dim view. As the law might. Using the mails to defraud, I'd imagine. Since *The American Cat Fancy* is distributed by mail. And since her advertisements were, of course, fraudulent."

"And Miss Arnold?"

"Probably Mrs. Cummins thought it likely that Barton had told her more than he did. That she might be a danger to be eliminated. The devout Mrs. Cummins is not long on scruples, I think. In fact, it is quite possible she was responsible for the death of her husband."

He told Susan about Randolph Cummins and the stipulation on which he had been released from medical supervision.

"No sexual activity," Susan said. "And our Mrs. Cummins knew about that?"

"She had been his nurse. Cummins was generally

198

thought to be very wealthy. Which, of course, is nothing the District Attorney of our county can bring up now."

"The cat in the car with Carol?"

"Mrs. Cummins didn't go to church Sunday. She waited at home for the sound of the crash she hoped she had arranged. She went down—it's only a few hundred yards—and rescued her cat."

"And thought the girl was dead?"

"Hoped so, anyway. Might have made sure, but a trooper came along. And maybe had another try Sunday evening, when she gave Carol a drink with a heavy dose of barbiturate in it. Also, I think, was trying to make up her mind to finish the job—and Carol —off this morning while I was telephoning the hospital. At least, it looked as though she was about to give the girl a lethal injection when I showed up. Carried a hypodermic around in her smock pocket, apparently just in case it might come in handy. I've no proof of that. In fact, I have some reservations. But it's Barton who's dead, of course."

"You mean you've got her there? On killing Barton?"

"We have plenty to hold her on suspicion of homicide," Heimrich said. "And we'll find more. When we know what to look for, we generally find it."

"And what was that you said about having reservations, dear?"

"Because why was she taking so long to kill Carol? She had her there two nights, all of Monday and into today, when I showed up. It looks to me as if she was vacillating. I'd guess that on Monday— while Carol was drugged—she drove Mrs. Evans's Volks down to White Plains and took a cab back. Was that only so the Volks would have no connection with

199

her? Or to provide us with a false lead while she—while she what? Maybe she found it's an entirely different problem to kill someone in your own house. Carol had presented herself there, and it could be Mrs. Cummins wasn't sure just what to do with her, once she had her. As an R.N. she must have known that all her talk of concussion—if Carol's body was in her house—was no guarantee against a postmortem. Oh, well, we may never know. Perhaps she just couldn't bring herself to kill Carol because Carol was so concerned about the little cat. Something she said gave me the impression that the girl's worry rather touched her. She does love her cats, I think."

"What *about* her cats, by the way?"

"Roger King. That's been arranged. He's a—well, a trained cat-sitter."

They finished their drinks. Susan picked up the tray and then put it down again.

"Speaking of cats," she said, "here comes ours."

Mite was coming toward the terrace, sauntering toward the terrace. A few yards from it he stopped to consider something. Then he came on. But on the terrace he began to retch. "Not another animal to another vet," Susan said. "Surely not."

"Just been eating grass, probably," Heimrich said. But there was concern in his voice.

Mite completed throwing up. It was grass, which cats use as an emetic.

Mite regarded the result without enthusiasism. He looked up at Susan. "You didn't have to wait until you got to the terrace, cat," Susan told him.

But Mite was not listening to her. He was listening, pointing toward, a more distant sound. Somewhere, at a considerable distance, a cat was screaming, in apparent agony.

200

But it did not sound like that to Mite. He knows the call of a female in season when he hears it. He went off the terrace, at a trot, at first. Then he went in bounds. Another tom might also be listening.

They watched their cat go.

"And no stud fee," Susan said, and picked up the tray.